A Tl

It was by now after six o'clock and the sun was beginning to sink in the sky and birds were going to roost.

But there were still plenty of butterflies hovering over the flowers and the soft buzz of bees collecting pollen.

The Count walked slowly over the green grass that was as soft as velvet.

He went towards the shrubbery and the cascade and then, as he passed by the entrance to the Herb Garden, he thought that he would take a look at the fountain.

It always pleased his artistic sense to see the water flung up in the air and then in the sunshine it looked like little drops of the rainbow as it fell into the bowl beneath it.

He walked through the gate and then stopped.

He had expected the Herb Garden to be empty as it usually was.

To his surprise someone else was there.

He saw that it was a woman who seemed to be part of the falling water and the sunshine turned her hair to gold.

It was someone had never seen before.

She was, however, so lovely and so much part of the fountain that he felt that he was looking at a painting by some great Master.

THE BARBARA CARTLAND PINK COLLECTION

Titles in this series

A TRAIN TO LOVE

BARBARA CARTLAND

Barbaracartland.com Ltd

THE BARBARA CARTLAND PINK COLLECTION

Dame Barbara Cartland is still regarded as the most prolific bestselling author in the history of the world.

In her lifetime she was frequently in the Guinness Book of Records for writing more books than any other living author.

Her most amazing literary feat was to double her output from 10 books a year to over 20 books a year when she was 77 to meet the huge demand.

She went on writing continuously at this rate for 20 years and wrote her very last book at the age of 97, thus completing an incredible 400 books between the ages of 77 and 97.

Her publishers finally could not keep up with this phenomenal output, so at her death in 2000 she left behind an amazing 160 unpublished manuscripts, something that no other author has ever achieved.

Barbara's son, Ian McCorquodale, together with his daughter Iona, felt that it was their sacred duty to publish all these titles for Barbara's millions of admirers all over the world who so love her wonderful romances.

So in 2004 they started publishing the 160 brand new Barbara Cartlands as *The Barbara Cartland Pink Collection*, as Barbara's favourite colour was always pink – and yet more pink!

The Barbara Cartland Pink Collection is published monthly exclusively by Barbaracartland.com and the books are numbered in sequence from 1 to 160.

Enjoy receiving a brand new Barbara Cartland book each month by taking out an annual subscription to the Pink Collection, or purchase the books individually.

The Pink Collection is available from the Barbara Cartland website www.barbaracartland.com via mail order and through all good bookshops.

In addition Ian and Iona are proud to announce that The Barbara Cartland Pink Collection is now available in ebook format as from Valentine's Day 2011.

For more information, please contact us at:

Barbaracartland.com Ltd.
Camfield Place
Hatfield
Hertfordshire AL9 6JE
United Kingdom

Telephone: +44 (0)1707 642629
Fax: +44 (0)1707 663041
Email: info@barbaracartland.com

THE LATE DAME BARBARA CARTLAND

Barbara Cartland who sadly died in May 2000 at the age of nearly 99 was the world's most famous romantic novelist who wrote 723 books in her lifetime with worldwide sales of over 1 billion copies and her books were translated into 36 different languages.

As well as romantic novels, she wrote historical biographies, 6 autobiographies, theatrical plays, books of advice on life, love, vitamins and cookery. She also found time to be a political speaker and television and radio personality.

She wrote her first book at the age of 21 and this was called *Jigsaw*. It became an immediate bestseller and sold 100,000 copies in hardback and was translated into 6 different languages. She wrote continuously throughout her life, writing bestsellers for an astonishing 76 years. Her books have always been immensely popular in the United States, where in 1976 her current books were at numbers 1 & 2 in the B. Dalton bestsellers list, a feat never achieved before or since by any author.

Barbara Cartland became a legend in her own lifetime and will be best remembered for her wonderful romantic novels, so loved by her millions of readers throughout the world.

Her books will always be treasured for their moral message, her pure and innocent heroines, her good looking and dashing heroes and above all her belief that the power of love is more important than anything else in everyone's life.

"I have always loved the beauty of Italy, its glorious Churches, its fabulous views and its sublime paintings that show throughout history that the power of love is still more important than anything else in everyone's life."

Barbara Cartland

CHAPTER ONE
1884

"What do you intend to do about the house?" the Earl of Kencombe asked.

There was a distinct pause before Lola answered,

"I thought maybe, Uncle Arthur, I could stay here."

"Stay here alone?" the Earl exclaimed, "of course not! You know as well as I do a girl of eighteen cannot live alone, unless you can find someone to chaperone you."

Lola had already thought of this and she had to say rather weakly,

"I cannot think of anyone I would not have to pay."

That she knew was the crucial point.

She had known when she saw the expression on her uncle's face that their discussion, when they did have one, was going to be very difficult.

She had just buried her father and mother.

It seemed incredible that only a few days ago they were all so happy in the small village in Worcestershire.

They had few neighbours, but that had not worried them and Lola could not imagine any two people being as happy as her father and mother.

Granted that all her mother's family had violently disapproved of her marriage.

Lady Cecilia Combe had been very beautiful and her parents were looking forward to presenting her at Court and giving her a Season in London.

To their horror, just before they were packing up to leave their house in Norfolk, Lady Cecilia had announced that she wished to marry her brother's Tutor.

Neville Fenton was a gentleman, but apart from that he had little to recommend him to the family.

He was very clever and had had a good education and he had started to write books after they were married. These were acclaimed as being brilliant, but did not bring in a great deal of money.

His books were usually on rather obscure subjects that few people found especially interesting, but to his wife they were everything she wanted to read and hear.

Lady Cecilia's father was furious at her persisting that Neville Fenton was the only man she would marry.

He threatened to cut her off without a penny, but, when they were actually married, he relented to give her Government Stock that brought her in fifty pounds a year.

This, Lola knew, was all that she had now to live on, dress and feed herself and keep a roof over her head.

She suspected that if anyone from the family did come to the funeral it would be her uncle, who had recently inherited the title.

She was well aware that her mother had never been very fond of him and they had not got on well.

Her younger brother, to whom Neville Fenton had been Tutor, had sadly died when he was only eighteen.

Even as Lola was watching the two coffins being lowered into the grave, she had found it difficult to believe that her father and mother had really left her.

They had only gone on a short railway journey to Worcester.

Her father had wanted more manuscript paper and to explore the bookshops, as he always hoped to find books of reference for his next book.

That they had been involved in a railway accident on their return journey seemed incredible.

It was not as though it was a very serious accident, with only three people having been killed.

But two of them had been her father and mother.

It was one of those accidents that were inevitably taking place on the new railways that were being built all over England and the Companies boasted that there were very few accidents and if they did they were not serious.

Nothing could be more serious to Lola, however, than to lose her adored father and mother.

She suddenly found herself an orphan with no one to turn to for help except her mother's family, which meant the fifth Earl of Kencombe.

She had notified him of her parents' deaths.

When he had actually appeared in the small village Church, she felt her heart sink.

He was looking just as supercilious as she expected he would and he was, in his own way, very overpowering.

They had come back after the Service to the pretty Elizabethan cottage which was her home.

Lola felt that he looked disdainfully at the small rooms, the ancient casements and the sparse furniture.

No one could have said that Meadow Cottage was anything but attractive, but Lola knew instinctively that to her uncle size counted more than beauty.

He had found it hard to believe that his sister could prefer a cottage to the mansions that had been inhabited by the Earls of Kencombe for five generations.

He walked across the room now in a few strides and stood looking out at the garden.

Lady Cecilia had made it a picture of beauty every spring and summer and she had tended it all herself, just as she had the Herb Garden and everyone admired it.

Lola knew that her uncle was thinking of his broad acres, a huge Park with stags and the pastures her mother had ridden high-spirited horses over as a girl.

Lady Cecilia had described it all to her daughter so often that Lola felt that she had lived there herself and she could picture everything her mother had done until she lost her head to the most attractive man she had ever seen.

Neville Fenton was certainly that, but unfortunately his handsome looks could not provide him with money and the only way he could make any was to tutor for Oxford and Cambridge examinations.

As he often boasted, his students always succeeded, thanks to the coaching they had received from him.

Between the two, who ordinarily would never have met each other, there was an instant affinity and they both acknowledged that it was love at first sight.

All they had to live on was Lady Cecilia's fifty pounds a year and what Neville Fenton could make out of the books he now began to write as well as his tuition fees.

He fortunately inherited Meadow Cottage from his grandmother, who had retired there when she was a widow and to him and his wife it was a little Paradise of their own and they asked for nothing more.

They could only afford one horse between them, but, as Lady Cecilia was such a good rider, she was often mounted by the local Master of the Foxhounds because, as he often boasted, he had known her father.

Actually it was because she was so pretty and charming that she graced any hunting field just by being present.

4

When she and her husband were riding together, it was said that no two people could look more attractive. It was as if they came from some abode of the Gods.

'Lola' was an abbreviation of the Spanish name, Dolores, and, when she was born, her father was writing a book about Spanish customs.

She was small, slim and very lovely. And she had the same fair hair as Lady Cecilia and the very dark blue eyes of her father.

Neville Fenton had often been told that his eyes were like a tempestuous sea, but on Lola they looked more like the Madonna's robe and they accentuated the fairness of her skin and her exquisitely chiselled classical features.

"You are so very lovely, my darling," Lady Cecilia said to her daughter on her eighteenth birthday. "I wish that Papa and I could give a ball for you."

"I am more than happy to dance with Papa while you play the piano," Lola had answered her.

Her mother smiled, but Lola realised that she was disappointed, as she really wanted her daughter to have the same advantages that she had enjoyed and her family had declared that she had thrown those advantages away.

"If only we had a little more money," she had said once when they could not afford to buy something that she particularly wanted.

Then, before Lola could speak, she had added,

"What a silly thing to say! I have everything in the world, in fact no woman is richer than I am."

She kissed her daughter and then on an impulse she had gone into the study and kissed her husband. She told him that she loved him even though she was disturbing him when he was working.

'How can they have left me?' Lola silently asked again for the hundredth time.

"I suppose," the Earl said in a harsh voice, "I shall have to look after you and you will have to come and live with me at Kencombe Hall."

"That is very kind – of you," Lola replied faintly.

At the same time every single nerve in her body was crying out that she had no wish to go there.

It was what she would have to do, but she wanted to stay here in this lovely cottage that was so filled with sunshine and love.

Her mother had often spoken of her family home, but she had, however, always been reserved when talking about her elder brother.

Now that Lola had seen him, she realised that her instinct in guessing that he was unpleasant was right.

"Of course you can make yourself useful about the house," the Earl was saying, "and I daresay your aunt will find quite a number of tasks to keep you busy."

Lola pressed her lips together.

She could imagine all too well how, because she was unwanted, that she would be made a jack-of-all-trades and every task that no one else was willing to do would be assigned to her.

"Well, that's settled," the Earl said, "I suppose you have enough money to bring you to London."

He hesitated a moment before he went on,

"There is no one here to travel with you, so you will have to do that part of the journey alone. But I will arrange for one of the housemaids at Kencombe House in Park Lane to accompany you to my house in the country. I am not certain of the train service, but, if you have to stay one night in London, the servants will look after you."

"Thank you, Uncle Arthur," Lola said demurely.

She was thinking that, if he could keep up the large house in London and an even larger one in the country, he could easily afford to give her a small allowance.

Then she could stay here and engage a chaperone to look after her and she was sure she could find an elderly retired Governess and so she would not have to continually hear her relations telling her what a mistake her mother had made in marrying her father.

Lady Cecilia had only received a few letters from her family and they had always hinted that she had made a terrible mistake in her life.

Lady Cecilia had read the letters and laughed.

"They really don't understand," she had said to her husband. "If I was offered Buckingham Palace, the Shah of Persia's Palace and the Taj Mahal, I would still choose Meadow Cottage as long as you were with me."

Neville Fenton kissed his wife and declared,

"I love and adore you, my darling, and nothing else is of any consequence."

"Nothing," Lady Cecilia agreed, "except our little angel who is going to grow up just as clever as you are."

"And as long as she is as beautiful as you," Neville Fenton said, "no one will bother about her brains!"

Now Lola told herself,

'If I really had any brains, I would manage to stay here at Meadow Cottage.'

She was only too well aware, however, that, even if she could afford to do so, her uncle would never allow it. Not that he wanted her to be with him and his family, but he would worry about what 'people would say'.

Lady Cecilia had been well known and liked in the County and they would certainly disapprove if her only child was to be neglected by the Kencombes.

"That means I shall expect you on Wednesday," the Earl was saying.

He was speaking rather louder than necessary as if he was determined to make sure that she would obey him and Lola could only reply weakly,

"I will pack everything up and bring with me what I wish to keep."

"Then you had better put the house up for sale," the Earl asserted.

Lola hesitated and then told him the truth.

"Well actually, Uncle Arthur, a very good friend of Papa's, who is a retired Don from his College at Oxford, has asked if I would rent it to him."

"You did not tell me that before," the Earl said angrily. "You said that you wished to stay here yourself."

"That is what I would still like to do."

"Well, you cannot do so and therefore there is no more argument about it. I am your Guardian and, whether you like it or not, you have to obey me."

"I have already said, Uncle Arthur, that I will come to you on Wednesday."

He was bullying her and she hated him for it.

At the same time, because she could not bear to part with the cottage where she had been so happy, she would rather it was looked after by her father's friend.

He had promised he would take care of the books and furniture, which would be better than selling them.

"What rent would he pay?" the Earl demanded.

"Thirty pounds a year and I know that he will be very careful with everything."

"Thirty pounds!" the Earl said reflectively. "Well, with the fifty pounds from your mother, you will be able to pay for your clothes and anything else you may require."

He paused for a moment and then added,

"You will have your food free with me and a roof, a very substantial one, over your head. In fact you are a very lucky young woman."

Lola forced herself to reply,

"I am, of course, very grateful, Uncle Arthur."

"Then that is all settled. Now I must leave for the station. There is a train in half an hour if it is punctual."

He walked out of the sitting room into the small hall. His top hat was on a chair and he picked it up.

Outside the front door the carriage he had hired to bring him from the Station to the Church was waiting.

When the driver saw Lola, he touched his forelock.

"Nice to see you, Miss Lola," he said. "It's sorry I be about your father and mother. They'll be real missed in these parts."

"I miss them terribly," Lola murmured.

Her uncle climbed into the carriage and she went to the open window to say,

"Goodbye, Uncle Arthur. It was very good of you to come. I know Mama would have appreciated it."

"Goodbye," the Earl replied, "and don't forget that I will be expecting you on Wednesday."

Lola stood back as the driver started up his horses.

She raised her hand to wave, but was aware that her uncle was staring straight ahead.

She watched the carriage drive through the wooden gate and then she turned and ran into the house.

She had kept tight control of herself all through the service and while her uncle was there.

Now the tears were running down her cheeks.

Leaving the front door wide open, she went up to her bedroom and flung herself on the bed and, burying her face in the pillow, she cried and cried.

She felt that she had lost everything.

Not only her father and mother but her home and the happiness she had known ever since she was born.

She only wished that she had been with them in the train and that she had died too.

Really what was the point of living when there was nothing in the future but Uncle Arthur bullying her? And his family would scorn her because she was more or less a penniless orphan.

"Oh, Mama, Papa!" she sobbed, "how could you do this to me, how can I possibly go away to live with those horrible people who never cared for you?"

It was a long time later before she stopped crying.

She told herself that she must tidy the house and pack all the things that she wanted to take with her.

She wished she could take everything, especially the four-poster bed with its crisp muslin curtains tied back with little bows of blue ribbon that matched her eyes.

She wanted everything in her mother's room. It was all part of her life and the endless love her mother had given her.

She went downstairs into the small room her father had made his study and where he wrote his books and she looked at those lining the walls and could not bear to leave them behind.

Because Neville Fenton had always tutored boys, he had taught Lola in much the same way as he had taught them. She had learned Latin, French, Italian and a little Greek as well as all the usual subjects.

It was when she was staring at her father's books that Lola suddenly had an idea.

'Why should I not earn my living as Papa did?' she asked herself. 'I might be a Governess to children and why should I not write a book as he did.'

Her mother had often said that, if her father had had the time, he must write a book about herbs.

"People are just so foolish about their health," Lady Cecilia had said. "God has created for us all the plants to cure every ailment. But instead of using His bounty, we go to a doctor and swallow a lot of pills, which in my opinion often make us worse than we were before we took them!"

Neville Fenton had laughed.

"I will write a herb book for you, my darling," he said. "As soon as I have finished the one I am on now."

He had in fact finished his book the day before they had taken the train to Worcester and she just knew that it would not make much money, although it would receive rave reviews.

She was, however, certain that, if she was living at Kencombe Park, she would never be allowed to waste her time, as they would call it, in that frivolous way. Instead she would be given thousands of boring chores to do.

'What I must find,' she mused, working it out for herself, 'is a post where I can be paid for what I am doing, but it does not take up all my time.'

Once again she was thinking that perhaps she could become a Governess.

Then, because she was intelligent, she realised that she would be thought too young and, although it sounded rather conceited, too pretty.

Her mother had often laughed at the stories in the popular books of romance and how the tall good-looking

11

Nobleman had come ostensibly to marry the daughter of the house, but instead ran off with her Governess.

"I don't think that happens in real life," she had said. "I remember my Governesses were always extremely plain, rather dull and bitter women, who would have liked to be married but never had the chance."

"What happens to any pretty women who wants to be a Governess?" Lola had asked.

"No woman would ever want a pretty Governess in the house," her father said. "They would be a disturbing element, so the wise Mamas choose the plainest and dullest teachers for their children!"

'If I cannot be a Governess,' Lola now thought, 'what can I do?'

Then, almost as if in direct answer to her question, she remembered a recent conversation she had heard.

The Lord Lieutenant's wife had called in to see her mother a week or so ago.

They were talking about servants. An inevitable subject, Lola had thought, with people in the country and the Lord Lieutenant's wife was saying how difficult it was to get staff as the young all preferred to work in a town.

"I have been trying for months," she went on, "to find a new housekeeper as ours has retired."

"And you have not been successful?"

"I have been to the Agency in London," the Lord Lieutenant's wife replied, "Mrs. Hill in Mount Street. I expect you have heard of her. She says that housekeepers of the old sort, who run the house perfectly, do not exist."

"I can understand the difficulty," Lady Cecilia said sympathetically.

Lola was listening and saw that her mother's eyes were twinkling.

That was not surprising, for the only staff they had was old Betsy from the village. She came every morning to clean and tidy and she adored Lady Cecilia and tried to save her from any unnecessary work.

"Now don't you wash up after dinner, my Lady," she said often enough. "I'll do it in the mornin' and you just relax and enjoy yourself when you 'ave finished dinner with your 'andsome 'usband."

Lady Cecilia had smiled.

"That is what I love doing, Betsy. When we are sitting round the fire talking, I am happier doing that than going to the Opera or a huge ball at Devonshire House."

Lola was aware her mother was talking to herself rather than to Betsy, who had never heard of Devonshire House.

What that conversation had told her was the name of an Agency in London.

'The moment I arrive,' she decided, 'I will go and see if they have anything I can do.'

She gave a deep sigh.

'I will do absolutely anything rather than have to go to Kencombe Park and live with Uncle Arthur.'

Then because she was practical she realised that she would need a reference.

She settled at her father's desk and in her excellent handwriting she wrote references for all the different posts that she might be offered,

"*Lady Cecilia Combe strongly recommends Miss Lola Fenton who has taught her daughter for a year.*"

She then went on to say what an excellent character Miss Lola Fenton had and just how trustworthy she was in every possible way.

She read it again and thought that she still looked too young even to be a Nursery Governess.

'What else can I do?' she asked herself.

One thing she could do was to cook, as her mother had taught her all the special dishes, many of them French, that her father enjoyed so much.

So on another piece of paper she wrote,

"*Lady Cecilia Combe is happy to recommend Miss Lola Fenton as –* "

'I can also ride,' Lola thought, 'and groom a horse'.

It seemed unlikely that anyone would employ her in that capacity, but she would still have her reference ready.

She was wondering what else she could do, when suddenly she caught sight of the curtains.

A skill her mother had excelled in was embroidery. Lady Cecilia had sewed, as she said herself, almost before she could walk.

The Dowager Countess had taught her to embroider and mend the beautiful sixteenth century curtains that hung over the huge windows at Kencombe Park.

Lady Cecilia had taught Lola how to embroider the most intricate designs and had showed her how to mend damaged material until it looked almost new.

She was always looking for old satins and velvets that were often obtainable quite cheaply at auction sales.

"I am not going to buy new curtains," Lady Cecilia had declared. "When those in the dining room have to be replaced, I am going to find some old but pretty ones that are more in keeping with our cottage."

She had bought two sets of curtains very cheaply. To the onlooker they seemed worthless, worn and torn, but under Lady Cecilia's skilful hands and with Lola to help they had looked almost brand new.

'Of course I can do that,' Lola told herself now.

She had never thought that such a skill would be marketable, but another reference from Lady Cecilia was added to the rest.

She put the references tidily away into the bag she would be carrying when she went to London.

*

When Tuesday came, it was agony to say goodbye.

Her father's old friend had already taken over the cottage and he promised that he would keep everything as best he could and he had reassured Lola by engaging Betsy to come every day as she had always done.

"Now you take care of yourself," he said, "and any time you want to come back, your room is there for you."

"Do you mean that?" Lola asked.

"Of course I mean it," he answered. "So, if things become unbearable, just come home."

Impulsively she kissed him.

"I know it is what Papa would like you to tell me," she said, "and thank you very very much."

She climbed into the farm cart that was waiting to take her to the station. It belonged to the local farmer who brought them eggs and a chicken when they could afford one and he had offered to drive her to the station.

"I'll see," he said, "that you be in a carriage where you'll not be disturbed, Miss Lola."

"That's so kind of you, Farmer Brown," she smiled.

When she drove down the street sitting beside him, the whole of the village seemed to be out on the pavement waving her goodbye.

It was hard to keep back the tears as she passed the grocer, who had always given her an extra sweet when she went in with her mother.

She passed the Church where they had worshipped on Sundays and the village butcher where legs of ham were hanging up in his shop window.

It was almost impossible to see through her tears by the time they reached the end of the street and then, when they were in the country, she wiped them away, ashamed of her own weakness.

"Now don't go and upset yourself," Farmer Brown was saying. "If things don't go right, then you just come home and we'll find a place for you somehow."

It was what she wanted to hear, but it did not make her feel any less like crying.

When they reached the Station, she thanked Farmer Brown again and again.

He found a porter for her and instructed him to see her into a suitable carriage and she waved and waved until Farmer Brown had driven off and was out of sight.

'That is the end of my childhood,' Lola thought.

Then, almost as if her father was there beside her, she thought she heard him say,

"Not at all. It's the beginning of a new chapter."

Having found an empty carriage and having put her luggage in the van, the porter said,

"You goes straight through to London, Missie, and I'll try to see as you don't 'ave anyone unpleasant in the carriage with you."

"Thank you, that is very kind of you," Lola said.

"Now you cheer up," the porter went on. "I've got a daughter about your age and I don't want to see 'er goin' off alone to them big Cities. Things goes on there that I don't like to think about."

She thought that everyone was very kind, but she had no idea that it was because she was so pretty and so young that every man wanted to protect her.

Lola had felt rather guilty when she bought a First Class ticket, but she knew how uncomfortable the Second Class was and often overcrowded.

She felt, as she was alone, that her mother would expect her to travel First Class.

Her father's friend had paid her in advance for the first three months of his tenancy and this meant that for the time being at least she had some money in her purse.

'If I can earn just a little more,' she said to herself, 'and save and save every penny, I shall be able to go home and live in the cottage with a chaperone.'

The train drew into Paddington Station and it was only a quarter of an hour late and Lola was surprised as she had heard so many complaints about late trains.

Again, because she looked so young and forlorn, a friendly porter went to the guard's van for her luggage and there was quite a pile of it because Lola had packed her mother's clothes as well as her own.

Outside the station the porter found her a cab to take her to Kencombe House in Park Lane.

The cabby was obviously impressed by the address and said he knew where it was and when they reached Park Lane the house was exactly as she had expected it to be.

The cab drove into a small 'in and out' drive and the horse came to a stop outside a porticoed front door.

The door opened and she saw a butler waiting for her with two footmen in livery behind him.

She stepped down from the cab and the butler asked in a superior voice,

"Miss Fenton, I believe?"

"Yes," Lola answered.

"So the train must have been punctual, miss," the butler said stiffly. "Well, that's certainly unusual."

"I am afraid I have rather a lot of luggage," Lola said apologetically. "But I expect you know I am leaving my home to go and live at Kencombe Park."

"So I've been told," he replied. "The housekeeper, Mrs. Jones, is waiting to show you to your room."

Lola felt rather like a child who was being handed from one nurse to another.

Mrs. Jones, in rustling black silk with a chatelaine at her waist, greeted her politely.

She led Lola into what she saw was a small single bedroom and she guessed that the larger rooms were kept for more important or married guests.

"Now then miss, if you'll tell the maid," Mrs. Jones said, "exactly what you want for the night, there'll be no need to unpack anything that's not required."

Lola did as she was told and then, having tidied herself, went downstairs.

"Surely, miss, you'd like to take off your hat and coat," the housekeeper suggested.

"I have to see a friend who lives very near here," Lola replied.

As she reached the hall, she had to repeat this to the butler as he had asked if she would like a cup of tea earlier than usual.

"That is kind of you," she replied. "I had something to eat on the train, but I would love to have some tea when I return. I just wish to see a friend who lives nearby."

"Would you like one of the housemaids to come with you, miss?" the butler asked in a lofty tone.

"There is really no need," Lola said hastily. "My friend lives only a street away."

She had found a street map of London amongst her father's books and this told her where Mount Street was.

She saw that she only had to walk down Park Lane and take a turning to the left.

She left the butler, who obviously thought that it was incorrect for her to be walking about alone.

She then hurried along, finding it not too difficult to follow the map and then found herself in Mount Street.

Just halfway down the street she saw a notice board over a door in bold letters – *Mrs. Hill's Domestic Agency.*

The door opened onto some stairs and Lola went up them to the first floor.

She saw several chairs inside the door of a large room with three people sitting on them.

One was an elderly woman, who she thought might be a Governess and the other two were young men, who obviously came from the country.

At the far end of the room was a high desk and sitting behind it was a woman with bright red hair.

Lola walked up to her and for a moment the woman did not raise her eyes from the ledger she was writing in.

Then, when she did so, she saw Lola and said,

"Oh, I am sorry, madam, I did not realise that you were here."

Lola realised at once that Mrs. Hill assumed she was a prospective employer rather than an employee.

"I have been informed, Mrs. Hill," she began, "how wonderful you are at finding staff and I thought perhaps you were the one person who would be able to help me find employment."

Mrs. Hill stared at her in surprise.

"You wish to be employed?" she asked, as if it was something unusual.

"Lady Leighton, the wife of the Lord Lieutenant of Worcestershire, advised me to come to you," Lola replied.

"My father and mother have been killed in a train accident and I don't wish to live in the country any longer."

Mrs. Hill's rather hard expression softened.

"So you're an orphan."

"Yes – and with very little money."

"Well, that certainly is a tragedy," Mrs. Hill said. "But what, my dear young lady, do you think you can do? That, of course, is the important question."

"I have been thinking about that and I have some excellent references. But I think you might say that I am too young to be a Governess."

Mrs. Hill smiled.

"Much too young and much too pretty."

It was just what Lola was expecting, so she was not disappointed.

"I can cook," she said, "and I am good with horses and I can sew or rather embroider."

Mrs. Hill stared at her.

"Did you say embroider?"

"Yes, my mother taught me to embroider so that I can mend old curtains, bedspreads and cushions and, when I have finished, they really look like new."

"Well, if that's the truth," Mrs. Hill then exclaimed, "you are an answer from the Gods. I have been looking through my books this very moment for someone who can repair old tapestries, embroidered curtains and suchlike."

"You have a position I can fill?" she asked eagerly.

"Only if you are quite certain you are telling me the truth. The employer in question has had three different applicants on approval and informed me that they were all hopeless. He dismissed them immediately."

"I promise you I will not be dismissed unless he is blind," Lola said.

"He's not that. Now perhaps you will tell me your name and, of course, I'd like to see your references."

Mrs. Hill's voice sharpened appreciably now that she was getting down to business and Lola thought that, if she was not convincing, she would be shown the door.

"My name – is Lola Fenton."

While Mrs. Hill was writing this down, she opened her handbag and took out the reference that referred to her embroidery skills, being careful not to let Mrs. Hill realise that there were three other envelopes in her handbag.

She handed it to her and Mrs. Hill read it.

"Now what is Lady Cecilia Combe's family?" she asked. "I don't think I've heard of her before."

"She is the daughter of the Earl of Kencombe," she answered, "but unfortunately her Ladyship is in poor health and is now living abroad."

"That's why I have not heard of her."

There were a number of Society magazines beside the desk that Mrs. Hill obviously studied every week.

Just occasionally her mother had bought *The Lady* magazine and had laughed at the photographs in them.

"They all look so very stiff and pompous," she said. "That, my darling, is what the Social world does to you. You turn up your nose as with a bad smell and then tell everyone that you are more important than they are!"

"I cannot see you doing that, Mama."

"Of course not," Lady Cecilia said, "but my aunts and uncles were always trying to impress people with their rank and my father was a very proud man."

Lola thought her mother sounded a little wistful.

There was always that note in her voice when she talked about her father, who she had been very fond of and it had hurt her terribly when he had been so angry at her determination to marry Neville Fenton.

Mrs. Hill now handed the reference back to Lola.

"Well, her Ladyship does speak highly of you," she said, "but you seem too young to have acquired such skill in so short a time."

"I have been sewing for years," Lola told her, "and I love embroidery. I do it if only to amuse myself."

"We can try you on his Lordship. I only hope for my own sake as well as his that you are satisfactory."

"I will do my best," Lola promised.

"I'll get in touch with him, although I believe he is abroad and I'll let you know if he's prepared to see you."

Lola gave a little cry.

"That does not suit me at all. I cannot do that!"

"Why not?" Mrs. Hill enquired.

"Because, if I don't take a post from you this very moment, I shall have to leave tomorrow for Norfolk to live with one of my relations. I am sure that, once I have gone there, there will be no chance of my getting away."

Mrs. Hill stared at her.

"Do you really mean that?"

"I promise you it's the truth. My uncle is a very difficult man and, once I have moved into his house, I am quite certain that he will refuse to let me come to London."

"That certainly makes it very difficult," Mrs. Hill said, "and his Lordship's very disappointed that I've not been able to help him."

"Then do let me try," Lola begged her. "Perhaps I could stay in his house and I will write to my uncle and say that I am staying with friends."

She was thinking aloud and Mrs. Hill remarked,

"I would hope that there's nothing wrong in what you're doing."

"Not wrong, merely that my uncle thinks I am too young to work. But I so want to be independent. Please, please help me! He is a very determined man and I know that shall be so unhappy with him."

She spoke pleadingly and, after what seemed a long hesitation, Mrs. Hill said,

"Well, we'll give it a chance. After all, if, when his Lordship arrives, he doesn't think you're suitable, there'll be no bones broken and I shall just have to try again."

"Oh, thank you, thank you!" Lola cried. "Can I go wherever it is at once or perhaps tomorrow morning?"

She was thinking that tomorrow morning would be more difficult, as the carriage would be waiting to take her to the Station.

"I suppose if it really suits you it'd be just as well to go there now as at any other time," Mrs. Hill conceded. "They'll not be expecting you, so you must not blame me if you get a poor reception. At the same time they know what his Lordship feels about his sixteenth century beds and the state they're in."

"I am sure I can make them look like new."

"I hope you're telling me the truth," Mrs. Hill said. "I want to believe you, but equally I'm a bit doubtful."

"I can understand that," Lola smiled, "and thank you so much for helping me. I shall always be grateful."

"Touch wood," Mrs. Hill said. "His Lordship may have very different ideas from yours."

"Not where embroidery is concerned!"

Mrs. Hill was already writing on a card.

"Now here's his Lordship's name and the address where you have to go. As you see, on the other side it says that I've sent you on a trial to attend to his requirements."

Lola took the card from her.

"Thank you," she sighed. "I can never be grateful enough for what you have done for me."

Because she spoke with such sincerity, Mrs. Hill smiled at her.

"Well, if you fail, you'd better come back and I'll see if I can find you a place as a cook."

"It sounds tempting, but I prefer the embroidery," Lola replied.

Mrs. Hill smiled at Lola again and it was obviously something she did not do very often.

Then, as Lola walked briskly to the door, Mrs. Hill wondered whether she had made a mistake.

'The girl's much too young,' she thought.

However, there was a fair chance that she might fit the bill and she wanted to please the Marquis.

CHAPTER TWO

When Lola was outside, she looked at the card Mrs. Hill had given her to make quite certain where the Marquis of Halaton lived.

It was in Grosvenor Square.

She set off, praying as she went that she would be successful. She was well aware that the Marquis would find it hard to believe, as she looked so young, that she could do such difficult embroidery.

She wondered if she put on her hat in a different way or if she wore spectacles that she would look older.

Then she laughed at herself. What was the point of pretending when he would soon realise that she was not as old as she had made herself look?

'I must just hope,' she thought. 'Otherwise it will be Uncle Arthur and misery!'

She found Halaton House easily on the far side of the Square and, as she expected, it looked very impressive.

She paused for a moment before she rang the bell.

She was saying a quick prayer, not only to God but to her mother and father that they would help her, as they would know how terrible it would be to be incarcerated in Kencombe Park, from where there would be no escape.

The door was opened by a footman and, before she could speak, an elderly butler came forward.

Quickly, just in case he mistook her for an ordinary caller, Lola said,

"I have been sent by Mrs. Hill with regard to the embroideress I understand his Lordship requires."

The butler looked surprised, but he replied calmly,

"In which case, miss, then you'll need to see Mrs. Whicker, the housekeeper. Kindly come this way."

She followed him across the hall and then he sent a footman to take her by a side staircase to the first floor.

Halfway up the stairs the footman turned and said,

"If you're lookin' for a position, you couldn't do better than be with these people, they're real nice, I can say that for 'em."

Lola realised he was being friendly and answered,

"Thank you for telling me. I am very anxious to take up the position, so I hope they will engage me."

At the top of the stairs the footman added,

"I wish you luck."

She thought he had an admiring look in his eyes and then he knocked on a door.

A voice called out "come in."

He opened the door and announced,

"A young woman to see you, Mrs. Wicker."

Lola entered the room and knew at once that it was the housekeeper's room as her mother had described the one at Kencombe Park to her.

There was a round table in the centre of it where the senior servants had their meals and there was also a sewing machine and a large work-basket in a corner of the room.

An elderly woman dressed in black was sitting in a comfortable armchair.

Opposite her was another woman of the same age, dressed identically, but with a silver chatelaine at her waist.

As Lola went towards them, the first woman, who she knew was looking at her critically, said,

"Have you come from Mrs. Hill's Agency?"

"Yes, I have," Lola replied, "and she told me that you are looking for someone who can embroider sixteenth century curtains."

"Is that what you can do?" the woman asked. "You look far too young to be capable of that sort of work."

Lola opened her handbag.

She produced the reference she had written about her embroidery skills and gave it to her.

As she did so, the other woman piped up,

"If you were to ask me, Mrs. Whicker, his Lordship is expectin' too much. I don't believe that anyone today can do that kind of work."

"I'd expect you're right, Mrs. Field," Mrs. Whicker replied. "But on his Lordship's instructions we still have to go on tryin'."

She was reading Lola's reference as she spoke and then somewhat reluctantly she remarked,

"Her Ladyship certainly praises you highly. Can it be possible you could do this very intricate embroidery?"

"I have done it on a great number of curtains that were Elizabethan," Lola replied, "and all I ask is that you give me a chance to show you what I can do."

Mrs. Field gave a laugh.

"No one can say fairer than that, Mrs. Whicker, and you may be in for a surprise."

"It would certainly surprise me if she can," Mrs. Whicker retorted.

She read the reference once again and then handed it back to Lola and, as she did not speak, Lola insisted,

"Please, please give me a trial. But a problem is that, if you cannot allow me to come to you either tonight or tomorrow morning, I have to go to Norfolk to stay with some relations and I may never have the chance of coming to London again."

"That makes it very difficult for me," Mrs. Whicker said, "for the simple reason that his Lordship is abroad and I can't consult him as to whether or not to employ you."

Lola's heart dropped.

"In that case," she sighed in a low voice, "I suppose I will have to give up hoping."

"You don't want to go to live with your relations?" Mrs. Field asked. "Why not?"

"They don't really want me. They were very angry when my mother ran away with my father and they have only communicated with me because I am now an orphan."

"Your father and mother are dead?" Mrs. Whicker asked. "How can that have happened?"

"They were killed – in a railway accident."

She could not help her voice breaking as she spoke or the tears coming into her eyes.

"That must have been a terrible tragedy for you," Mrs. Whicker said kindly. "Now do sit down, my dear, and let's talk about it."

Lola was aware that her attitude had changed.

She wiped her eyes and sat down on a hard chair.

"I see that your name," Mrs. Whicker said, "is Lola Fenton and you look very young to me."

"I am nearly nineteen and I promise you that I can embroider just as well as Lady Cecilia says I can."

"If you'll take my advice," Mrs. Field intervened, "you'll give the girl a trial. It won't be any bones off your back if she fails and she won't be the first or the last."

"Well, I suppose you're right," Mrs. Whicker said. "But I don't want to disappoint his Lordship by showin' him again the appallin' mess that last woman made. I had to unpick it all meself. I couldn't trust anyone else."

"I promise you," Lola chimed in, "that you will not have to unpick anything I have done. I only wish that you could see the Elizabethan curtains that I repaired for Lady Cecilia. Everyone said they looked just like new and were too beautiful to be so old."

"She can't say better than that, can she?" Mrs. Field remarked.

"I'm takin' a risk," Mrs. Whicker said, "and, if you disappoint me, young woman, I shall just give up and his Lordship'll have to find new curtains and forget the old ones."

"It'd break his heart," Mrs. Field added, "you know that. He wants everythin' perfect."

"Which he's not likely to get in this world," Mrs. Whicker added.

"So you will engage me?" Lola murmured.

Surprisingly Mrs. Whicker smiled at her.

"I always was a bit of a gambler, so I'm bettin' on an outsider."

Lola clapped her hands together.

"Thank you, thank you!" she cried. "I am so very grateful. Will I be working here?"

Mrs. Whicker shook her head.

"No, my dear, the curtains are in the country and, as I'm leavin' tomorrow mornin', you can travel with me."

"You are very kind," Lola said.

As she spoke, she was thinking that somehow she would have to get away from Kencombe House with her luggage without anyone knowing where she was going.

She ruminated for a moment and then she said,

"Will it then be possible for me to come here in the morning in a Hackney carriage with my luggage?"

"Yes, of course," Mrs. Whicker said, "but I wish to leave at nine o'clock, so don't be late."

"No, I will not be late and thank you again. I will not disappoint you."

Lola rose to her feet as she spoke.

Mrs. Whicker held out her hand.

"I shall expect you to be here at a quarter to nine," she said. "Your luggage'll go in the brake, so the sooner you're here the better."

"I understand and thank you once again."

She went to shake hands with Mrs. Field, who said,

"Now you take good care of yourself, my dear, and you'll be ever so happy in the country with Mrs. Whicker. She expects the best, but she has a heart of gold."

She looked at the other housekeeper with a smile and a twinkle in her eyes, as she asked,

"Isn't that true?"

"I hope so," Mrs. Whicker replied. "It's not always easy workin' for his Lordship, who expects too much."

Lola walked outside and was just shutting the door when she heard Mrs. Field say,

"Now what's a lady – for she definitely is one – takin' on a job like this for?"

Lola did not dare to wait to hear anything more, so she ran down the stairs and into the hall.

There was no sign of the butler and the footman on duty was the one who had taken her upstairs.

He smiled, opened the door for her and she slipped out.

As she walked away her heart was singing.

She had won, she had escaped from Uncle Arthur!

Unless she was ignominiously sacked, she might be able to stay with the Marquis for quite a long time.

When she reached Kencombe House, she ran up the stairs to find Mrs. Jones.

"You've been a long time with your friends, miss," she said. "I should have sent someone with you."

"I was fine," Lola replied, "and I shall not require the housemaid to go with me tomorrow morning because I am going to stay with my friends in the country."

Mrs. Jones looked surprised.

"I don't know what his Lordship'll say to that," she said. "He's expectin' you at Kencombe Park."

"I know, but as he does not particularly want me, I think he will be relieved that I have some friends I can stay with for a short time. I will write a letter to Uncle Arthur, otherwise he will wonder why I have not arrived."

Mrs. Jones showed her into a boudoir on the same floor and there on the desk was some writing paper bearing the Kencombe Crest.

Lola took off her hat and coat and thought carefully before she began to write,

"Dear Uncle Arthur,

I came to London as you told me to and found when I arrived that some friends have asked me to stay with them for a short while in the country.

I know you will understand that I feel it will give me a chance to recover from the shock of my father's and mother's deaths before I come to you.

Thank you so very much again for your kind offer to look after me. I will let you know when I am coming.

31

Again my gratitude for your kindness,
Lola."

She knew she ought to have put, '*your affectionate niece*', but somehow could not pretend even on paper that she had any affection for him.

She had escaped for a while from Kencombe Park, at least as long as she was efficient at her embroidery,

'Thank you, thank you, Mama and Papa,' she said softly in her heart.

She felt sure that they had guided her to Mrs. Hill and from Mrs. Hill to Mrs. Wicker.

She had not forgotten what the footman had said and thought that it was unlikely that any servant working for her uncle would speak so warmly of him.

When she had finished writing her letter and put it into an envelope, she rang the bell and a maid came.

"Will you please take this to the butler," she said, "and ask him to post it at once to his Lordship. It would be best if it could be sent tonight."

"I'll tell him, miss," the maid answered, "and they wants to know downstairs if you'll have your dinner in the dining room or on a tray in your bedroom?"

"As I am very tired," Lola said, "I would be very grateful if I could have it in my bedroom."

The maid disappeared with the letter and Lola went to her bedroom.

She would have liked to ask for a bath, but, as the servants had not offered her one, she did not want to cause a commotion.

She therefore washed in warm water from a highly polished brass can that had been placed on the washstand and, putting on one of the pretty nightgowns her mother had made for her, Lola climbed into bed.

It had been a long day and she really was feeling tired, but she did realise, however, that she was hungry.

Then her dinner was brought in by a footman.

There was a soup, some slices of lamb and a rather dull pudding consisting of under-ripe fruit in heavy pastry. She would not complain about anything now that she was spared from having to leave tomorrow for Kencombe Park.

And as soon as her dinner tray had been taken away she turned out the lights and went to sleep.

She had told the maid that she wanted to be called at half past seven with her breakfast and she was certain, as they served a martinet like her uncle, that they would be punctual.

*

She slept peacefully until about seven o'clock.

Then, excited at the thought of going to the country with Mrs. Whicker and frightened in case anything should prevent it at the last minute, she got up and started to dress.

She had packed and was ready for her breakfast by half past seven and she then decided that there was little point in waiting any longer.

She asked one of the footmen in the hall to find a Hackney carriage for her and then the butler asked her,

"Your friends are not calling for you, Miss Lola?"

"No. They have so much to arrange that I said I would go round to their house."

She thought that he looked disapproving, just as her Uncle Arthur would have done.

The Hackney carriage duly arrived and her luggage was piled on top and some put inside with her.

The coachman drove off and asked Lola where he was to go.

"Number 15 Grosvenor Square," she said in a low voice.

She started thinking about the Marquis of Halaton and, as he was so fussy about his curtains, Lola was certain that he was elderly, much older even than her uncle.

Although she had never heard of him, she supposed that, even if he was not important in politics, he would be well known because of his title.

'At least I am free for the moment,' Lola thought, 'and if I am dismissed or have to leave for some reason or other, I may be lucky and find somewhere else to go.'

She knew that she was being optimistic and at the same time she was trying to save herself from being too upset and unhappy if things went wrong.

Somehow she was sure that it was her father and her mother who had helped her escape from Uncle Arthur.

And she was not really alone in a frightening world, because they were near her.

*

The Marquis of Halaton was announced in a loud voice by the butler.

His friend the Count Camilo di Kalman jumped up from the comfortable chair he had been reclining in.

"Kelvin!" he exclaimed. "You are back and I am delighted to see you."

"I am back and exhausted," the Marquis said, "so give me a drink and then tell me all the appalling things our friends have been doing while I have been away."

The Count laughed.

"Why appalling?"

"Because you will always tell me the worst stories first," the Marquis replied, "and keep the good news for a savoury at the end of the meal!"

The Count laughed again and poured the Marquis a glass of champagne.

"Was it really an exhausting journey?" he asked.

"It was really ghastly. The sooner that something is done about the train service across Germany the better."

"I heard that they have improved it quite a lot," the Count said, "but it will never be enough to please you."

"Not unless I can get my own way," the Marquis replied.

He sat down in a comfortable armchair and looked enquiringly at his friend.

Count Camilo di Kalman was a diplomat and a very close friend of the Marquis of Halaton. They had often travelled together on the Continent.

Only the Count was aware how much the Marquis relied on him to make a secret dream come true.

Now, as he sipped his champagne, he said,

"You are deliberately keeping me waiting, Camilo, and you know that I have been thinking of you all the time I was crossing an unpleasantly rough Channel."

"Then you can cheer up, I have found exactly the man you want and I will now tell you all about him."

"In France?" the Marquis questioned.

"In Italy," the Count replied.

"And he will really do what I want?"

"He is delighted at the idea, but you will find him somewhat difficult."

"I just don't mind how difficult he is as long as he does what I want and as soon as possible."

"Well, that is what I think he will do," the Count said. "At least I have paved the way for you, Kelvin, and opened the door."

"For which I am extremely grateful."

The Marquis was a very rich man and he had been pandered to all his life by being able to have everything he wanted, almost before he asked for it.

When he was a small boy, he had become obsessed with trains.

As he had grown older, he had realised, as railways began to be such an essential part of the modern world, just how undependable they mostly were.

He then became completely convinced that the only railway system that could be efficient on the more difficult and dangerous routes must be electrified.

He had with great determination designed what he thought would be the most effective and certainly the most original electric engine.

As quite a lot of railways were privately owned, he could have floated his own railway Company and produced the electric train himself.

The Marquis, however, was exceedingly conscious of his exalted position in the Social world and his family was traditionally in attendance on Her Majesty the Queen.

His growing interest in trains would have shocked his uncles, aunts, cousins and other relations.

They would proudly point to the Halaton Coat of Arms and read the history of their ancestors' achievements through the centuries. They had been Statesmen, soldiers, sailors and advisers to Kings and Queens.

None of them, the Marquis knew only too well, had ever sunk to being in trade and to make money by having something to sell!

Having invented his electric engine, he then wanted more than he had ever wanted anything in his life to see it running on the rails throughout Europe.

He had come to the conclusion that there was only one way that this could be achieved.

It was for his invention to be taken up in another country rather than in England and the person he sold it to must be prepared not to divulge his connection with it.

The one confidant of his who had shared his secret was his great friend, Count Camilo di Kalman.

The Marquis had travelled abroad quite recently to investigate other railway systems on the Continent, while the Count had gone to Italy.

He and the Marquis were well aware that Italian railways were inferior to those in other countries.

This was not simply due to their negligence, but to the fact that the country itself was so exceedingly difficult to build a railway on. There was the great sweep of the Alps across its Northern frontier and the Apennine chain ran down the centre.

As one man had said to the Count,

"It may be Paradise for some people, but it is hell for railway engineers!"

There were endless steep gradients, winding routes and many tunnels and it was a nightmare for anyone who had anything to do with trains.

Italy had indeed achieved some measure of success with special mountain locomotives and the first had been built by an Austrian for the Upper Italy Railways in 1873.

They now, as the Count told the Marquis, had one hundred and six locomotives, but even that was not enough for such a large country.

"I will tell you one thing," the Count had said when they first talked about it. "The steam locomotives fill the many tunnels in Italy with choking smoke."

"I did not think of that," the Marquis had answered, "but I can understand it happening."

"It means," the Count went on, "that the number of trains allowed to pass through any tunnel during each hour has to be strictly rationed."

"Then what they need is electricity," the Marquis had said excitedly.

After that he began to design what he thought was the perfect electric train and, when he had finished it, he wanted to blow his trumpet and tell the world about it.

It was then that he realised how constricted he was by his social position and his family.

"You have to find me someone, Camilo," he said to the Count, "who will build my engine for me so that I can see it and enjoy it, but unfortunately in secret."

The Count had laughed at first, as he found it hard to believe that his friend was really serious.

Then, when they talked it over, he understood.

"Most of my family," the Marquis said, "abominate trains anyway. They are used to horses and so would do anything rather than have to travel in what to them is an uncomfortable, unpleasant and noisy vehicle."

"Then they don't know when they are well off!" the Count exclaimed.

To prove that the English trains were better than most, he had forced the Marquis to come to Italy with him.

"You must see," he said, "what the Italians have to put up with."

The Marquis found it appalling.

A typical coach on the Calabria-Sicilian Railway, which the Count insisted on showing him, was Third Class and had four wheels and it carried fifty passengers in five compartments separated by half partitions.

The seats were only one foot five inches wide and the whole coach was lit by just two oil lamps.

"Something must be done about your country," the Marquis commented.

"I agree," Camilo replied. "The best thing you can do would be to run a private railway system for us."

"It is what I would enjoy more than anything else, but sadly, as you know, I cannot possibly let anyone apart from you be aware of my secret hobby."

The Count had chuckled, yet he knew that what the Marquis was saying was the truth.

He was only half-Italian on his mother's side and his father was Hungarian and the combination had made him a very good diplomat.

Because he was very fond of the Marquis, he was determined to use all his powers to help him.

"I must say, Kelvin, you are certainly original," he said. "Most men would want me to introduce them to some alluring creature I have met on my travels."

He smiled as he went on,

"I have never met anyone before who preferred a puffing steam engine to a soft white body."

The Marquis's eyes twinkled.

"There is a time and place for everything," he said, "and I really don't want a steam engine in bed with me!"

"I should hope not," the Count replied. "As for so-called sleeping cars, they are extremely uncomfortable and that is something else you might redesign and improve."

"I shall be content with the engine for the moment."

"Well, I can only hope it is fast," the Count said. "I learnt on my last trip home that our fastest train averages under thirty miles an hour and the two hundred and eighty mile journey from Taranto to Reggio di Calabria, which as you know is located at the very heel of the country, took an exhausting sixteen hours at only seventeen miles an hour."

"Just wait until I get there," the Marquis then said complacently.

"It's not going to be easy," the Count warned, "to find the right person to manufacture your engine and to run a line it can travel on."

"If we build the engine first, we can then worry about the route, the speed and the carriages later."

He had gone abroad in order to see for himself what was happening in Germany and Hungary. Now he was at home and totally determined that however advanced those countries might be he could do better.

They sat talking for a long time about the engine and then, as the Count poured the Marquis another glass of champagne, he said,

"Now what do you intend to do? Shall I ask this man, whose name is Antonio Galvani, to come to England to see you or will you go to him?"

"I will go to him," the Marquis answered. "I have no wish for anyone here in London, except yourself, to have the slightest idea of what I am doing and you know how nosy women are."

The Count held up his hand.

"That reminds me. I have not yet told you that there is one snag about all this."

"What is that?" the Marquis asked.

"Antonio Galvani is prepared to build your engine and run the train in his name, but I must warn you that he is socially very ambitious."

"What do you mean by that, Camilo?"

"He is a very rich man and I am quite sure that he would not be doing this if you were not a Marquis and the head of one of the most important families in England."

The Marquis did not speak, but there was a twist to his lips and it told his friend all too clearly that he was used to being run after and it did not perturb him.

"What I am afraid you may find," the Count went on, "and I am only guessing, is that he will do everything in his power to make you marry his daughter."

"Oh, not another!" the Marquis groaned,

He was well used, because of his title and wealth, to have ambitious parents thrusting their daughters at him using almost any means to trap him into matrimony.

He had made up his mind a long time ago not to marry anyone until he was thirty or older.

Then he would require not one heir, but several to inherit his title and vast possessions.

He, in the meantime, enjoyed himself with exotic, sophisticated married women. They, as the Count had once said, fell into his arms like overripe peaches.

"You may think that I am being rather depressing on this subject," the Count was saying slowly, "but I had the distinct impression that Galvani will at the last moment refuse to build your engine for you without being bribed."

"With money?"

"With marriage," the Count replied.

"You just cannot be serious. After all, a man cannot force me to marry his daughter."

"No, but he can refuse to build the engine for you."

"Damn it all!" the Marquis exclaimed. "Surely one business should be kept apart from another."

"Not where Galvani is concerned. I heard quite a lot about him in the past when I was in Rome and he has gradually made himself an extremely influential man."

The Count saw that the Marquis was listening and he went on,

41

"You know how snobbish and stuck-up the Ducal and other ancient families in Italy are about blue blood. I am convinced, although, of course, I cannot prove it, that Galvani has tried to join himself, now that he is a widower, with quite a number of Rome's elite who, however, have shown him the door."

The Marquis did not speak and the Count added,

"So now he is concentrating on his daughter, who actually is extremely pretty."

"I don't care," the Marquis expostulated, "if she is as beautiful as Aphrodite or an Angel from Heaven, I have no wish to marry an Italian."

He was not being insulting to his friend. They had talked about this before and the Count accepted that the Marquis was totally convinced that the right person to be the future Marchioness of Halaton must be a pure blue-blooded English girl.

"Well, that is the position," the Count said. "I was thinking about it and I have decided that the best thing you can do now is to arrive in Italy with your fiancée."

"You are not serious?" the Marquis asked.

"I am indeed very serious, Kelvin. But, of course, an engagement can be broken and, even if your companion is your wife, she could be drowned at sea on the way back or lost in a Scotch mist!"

The Marquis laughed.

"Now you are talking nonsense! Could I possibly do either of those things?"

"I don't want to depress you," the Count said, "and naturally I may be wrong, but I have a feeling from various things Galvani said to me that he thinks you are Manna sent to him from Heaven. In other words exactly what he has been looking for."

"Then he will be disappointed."

"And so will you, Kelvin."

They sat there in silence for a moment before the Marquis rose to his feet.

"I will think over what you have said, Camilo. But, having raised my hopes and shown me the glittering star I so much wanted to see, you have now dragged me down into the depths of despair."

"I am sorry, old boy, but it is your own fault. You should not be so good-looking, so rich and so important. You well know that just to look at you makes every young woman smell orange blossom."

"Oh shut up! The whole idea makes me sick and you know how much I want my engine to be a reality and not just a drawing on paper."

"I do know," the Count said in a sympathetic voice, "so just listen to me for once. Think of someone you can take with you and immediately introduce to Galvani. You will then tell him you intend to marry her or are already married to her, it does not matter which!"

He hesitated and then continued,

"He will then realise from the very beginning that he cannot bargain with you over his daughter."

"The whole thing makes me very angry."

The Marquis strode towards the door.

"I am going home now to change for dinner," he said, "and I am expecting you at eight o'clock. I hope by then I shall be in a better temper."

"I hope so too," the Count smiled.

He did not escort the Marquis to the front door for more than one reason. They were such close friends that they used each other's houses as if they were their own and he knew that the Marquis's carriage was waiting outside.

He then took another sip of champagne and thought reflectively that by tomorrow morning the Marquis would have changed his mind.

He knew as no one else did how much the electric engine meant to him.

He was extremely clever and far too intelligent just to be a man about town or for that matter an ardent lover of a great number of beautiful women.

He had always wanted something very tangible to do, something he had to use his brain on and imagination and determination.

That was what had made him absolutely convinced that his particular design for an electric engine was exactly what the world wanted.

'He is indeed a most unusual person,' the Count told himself.

Unusual or not, the Marquis's handsome looks and vibrant personality would inevitably land him in trouble if there was a woman about – even if only on the horizon.

CHAPTER THREE

Lola and Mrs. Whicker travelled Second Class in a fairly comfortable carriage and luckily no one joined them.

When they arrived at the Halt, which was a special stop for the Marquis, there was a carriage waiting for them as well as a brake for their luggage.

Lola had not talked to Mrs. Whicker on the train for the simple reason that the wheels were very noisy.

Mrs. Whicker either dozed or had no wish to speak, so Lola looked out of the window and thought with much satisfaction that every mile carried her further away from Uncle Arthur.

The carriage that was waiting for them at the Halt was drawn by two fine horses that Lola longed to pat, but she felt, however, that it would be a mistake to do anything unusual and so she climbed into the carriage.

She had already told Mrs. Whicker that she came from the country and they talked about country people and country things and then they passed through a small village very like, Lola thought, the one at home.

They turned in through large iron gates embellished with gold and then, as they travelled up a drive lined with oaks, Lola had her first glimpse of the Marquis's house.

She gave an exclamation,

"It's Elizabethan!"

"Of course it is," Mrs. Whicker said, "I thought you knew that."

"I had no idea," Lola said, "but I can see it is built in the shape of an 'E' and I can recognise those lovely pink bricks that fade with age."

She was thinking of Meadow Cottage and it seemed to her a good omen that of all periods the house where she was going was Elizabethan.

"I should have thought," Mrs. Whicker said as they passed over an ancient stone bridge which spanned a lake, "that you'd have known from its name what period it was."

"Now I think of it. I have not heard the name. I should imagine that it would have been Halaton Hall."

Mrs. Whicker smiled.

"It's Queens Hoo and now you know which Queen it was named after."

"Queen Elizabeth! Did she actually stay here?"

"I believe that Her Majesty stayed here constantly because she liked riding and hunting in the woods. So now you can understand why his Lordship requires the curtains that were hung in her day to be properly restored."

"It's so exciting," Lola enthused, "and I can see that Queens Hoo is very beautiful and worthy of Royalty."

She did learn later that it had been considerably enlarged since it was first built and that Queen Elizabeth had only treated it as a Hunting Lodge.

The Halatons, who had later acquired the house and estate, had been very conscious of its first Royal owner and had kept as much as possible to the period.

When they reached Queens Hoo, Lola was thrilled with the huge hall, the narrow passages and the casement windows with their original diamond-shaped panes.

'It's almost like being at home,' she thought.

As the Marquis was not in residence, Mrs. Whicker was able to show her every room on the ground floor, then the State bedrooms on the first floor and the long Picture Gallery that had been added by the Marquis's grandfather.

Lola clasped her hands together when she saw the pictures. They had been collected over many centuries and added to, she was told, by the present Marquis.

"I could spend days just gazing at them," she said.

"But you must not forget, my dear," Mrs. Whicker smiled, "that you have to add to all these beautiful things."

"Yes, of course. I have not forgotten the curtains."

Mrs. Whicker took Lola to the Queen's room.

It was very large and was lit by two bow windows and they were hung with velvet curtains matching those on the bed that had a carved and gilt top to it.

The curtains once had been a bright pink and, like the bricks outside, they had faded to a soft romantic hue, which was very lovely and the curtains were embroidered with flowers, leaves and occasionally a small bird.

"They are beautiful!" Lola exclaimed.

"But look at this," Mrs. Whicker suggested.

She picked up a curtain and showed Lola how at the foot of it the velvet had been torn and the embroidery ruined. It might have been caused by a dog or perhaps by neglect she explained.

"His Lordship thinks that it was the washing," Mrs. Whicker said, "for, in Elizabethan days and long after, they washed the floors rather than polished them as we do."

"It has certainly made a mess of these curtains."

Lola was thinking while she gazed at them how she could repair the damage.

There was also wear and tear on those hanging on the bed and people, who had slept in it, must have pulled them roughly or pushed them behind the head-board.

47

Lola had arrived at Queens Hoo in time for a late luncheon that she and Mrs Whicker ate by themselves in the housekeeper's room.

When she had finished, Lola proposed,

"I think I should go and start work."

It was then that Mrs. Whicker had taken her around the house and, when she had shown her a great deal of it, she suggested that they should go into the garden.

"You are quite sure I am not neglecting my duties?" Lola asked.

"You can start work tomorrow mornin', my dear," Mrs. Whicker replied. "I think after a train journey, which I always find very tirin', you should get some fresh air and explore the cascade, the lily pool and the Herb Garden."

"I cannot wait to see them all and thank you for being so kind."

Lola ran off into the garden without a hat and Mrs. Whicker watched her go with a smile.

She thought there must be a story behind the fact that this beautiful child – for she seemed little more – was an orphan, penniless and having to earn her own living.

She could only hope that Lola was not exaggerating when she said that she could embroider and it would cheer the place up to have someone so young in it.

Lola explored the garden and found it as exciting as the house.

The cascade poured down through the trees to join a stream that flowed into a small lake and the lily pond was lovely with lilies coming into bloom and everything was so perfectly arranged and tended just as Lady Cecilia had tried to do in their garden.

Lastly the Herb Garden with its ancient Elizabethan walls, the fountain in the centre and the herbs growing in low beds was something that she had always wanted to see.

She had read about such gardens and helped her mother with the few herbs that they could afford to plant, but this was on a magnificent scale.

She went to stand by the exquisitely carved bowl of the old fountain and there were goldfish swimming in the water that fell from a cupid holding a large fish in his arms.

'It's lovely, lovely, lovely!' Lola was saying when she finally went back into the house.

She found herself repeating the same words when she went to bed that night.

*

The next morning she was determined to prove to Mrs. Whicker that she had been right to engage her.

She cleaned the velvet as her mother had taught her to do and stitched together the pieces that were torn and then she started to copy the pattern of flowers and leaves just as it was on that part of the undamaged curtain.

Mrs. Whicker explained that the embroideresses who had preceded her had always started by demanding a lot of expensive materials and then they had been unable to use them properly.

Lola was delighted with a sewing-basket filled with silks all carefully arranged, so that she could find the exact colour she wanted without any difficulty.

There were pink silks ranging from the faintest pink up to a dark red and there were blues, greens, yellows that ended in orange, whites, blacks, browns and every other colour in the rainbow.

She sat down on the floor and, once the velvet was clean and the tears had been repaired, she then started to embroider.

She was thinking as she did so of the Elizabethan women who had done the same three hundred years ago and it must have been gratifying for them that they were making the curtains beautiful for the Queen herself.

Lola must have been working for nearly two hours when Mrs. Whicker came into the room.

Lola looked up and smiled at her, realising from the expression on her face that this was the crucial moment, as Mrs. Whicker would now know if she had been right or wrong in engaging her.

"I have not done a great deal yet," she said, "but I hope you will agree this is an exact copy of the flowers."

Mrs. Whicker then looked closely at what Lola was showing her.

"It's excellent!" she cried. "I can hardly believe that you've actually done it yourself."

"Every stitch of it," Lola answered, "and, as you know, there will have to be a great many more."

Mrs. Whicker gave a deep sigh.

"I'm more relieved than I can say," she said. "I was so worried I'd made a mistake in bringin' you here."

"Now you need not worry anymore," Lola said. "I was telling the truth, was I not?"

"You're ever such a clever girl and I can't wait to see his Lordship's face when you show him what you've done."

Lola knew that Mrs. Whicker wanted her to have a lot to show him when he arrived, so she worked very hard.

She did, however, ask when he was expected and Mrs. Whicker made a gesture with her hands.

"We never know when his Lordship'll turn up," she answered. "He just likes to believe that everythin' goes on exactly the same whether he's here or not. Therefore he just appears without any warnin'."

"Surely that must be very difficult for the cook."

"Oh, his Lordship's a little more considerate when he's bringin' a party," Mrs Whicker said. "But, when it's just him and perhaps one of his friends, he walks in and expects, as I've told you before, perfection!"

Lola laughed.

"That is certainly asking a lot. If he has been like that all his life then he must have been often disappointed."

"Not so many times and, of course, we at Queens Hoo like to think we're the best!"

Lola laughed again and Mrs. Whicker added,

"Well, I needn't worry about you anymore. You go on as you are now and you'll be in the same category as the rest of us!"

"I shall be very honoured," Lola smiled.

She realised now that Mrs. Whicker had more or less adopted her since she had arrived at Queens Hoo.

For one thing, and she understood it was because Mrs. Whicker thought that she was a lady, she did not eat with the other servants.

It was usual for the butler, the housekeeper and the lady's maid to have their meals in the housekeeper's room.

Mrs. Whicker, however, arranged it that Lola had breakfast alone with her and also luncheon.

The servants had theirs at twelve o'clock and only when they had finished was Lola fetched from the Queen's bedroom.

She wondered on the first day what would happen for dinner and was not surprised when Mrs. Whicker said,

"As you'll often be workin' late and we have our supper at six-thirty, I'm goin' to arrange for you to have yours brought to your bedroom."

"I would like that," Lola replied, "because I want to have the chance of going into the garden before it gets too dark. My Mama always insisted that, when we had been embroidering for a long time, we needed some fresh air."

"Your mother be quite right," Mrs. Whicker said, "and that's what you'll do here."

Lola thought that this had made things much easier.

Although the servants were helpful and pleasant to her, they were not at all familiar in their attitude and they accepted that there was a barrier between her and them.

Anyway it was a joy to be anywhere as lovely as Queens Hoo.

And to wake up in the morning knowing that she would not have to face Uncle Arthur's disapproval or find herself resenting his criticism of her father and mother.

'I am very lucky,' she thought, 'and also, although I did not expect it – happy.'

*

The Marquis had intended to go to Queens Hoo as soon as he arrived back in London.

His secretary had left his correspondence waiting for him on his desk in the study of Halaton House.

Among it was a letter from one of the beauties who had attracted his attention before he left and she told him that she was longing to see him.

As her husband was going away to Newmarket for the races, she hoped, if it was possible, that they could dine together either at his house or hers.

The Marquis knew exactly what this meant and, as the writer was extremely beautiful, he thought it would be a pity to waste such an opportunity.

He therefore stayed in London and dined one night at her house and on the second night she came to his.

They were very discreet and there were no gossips to talk about them behind their backs or announce that a new *affaire de coeur* was developing.

The beauty's husband sent her a message when the races were over that he would not be returning for several more days.

The Marquis enjoyed himself, but he was almost relieved when the beauty informed him that her husband was now expected home the following day.

"I do love you, Kelvin," she purred, "and you have made me very happy."

It was the sort of statement that he had heard many times before and he responded as was expected of him.

"I cannot bear to lose you," she went on, "and we must meet somehow if only for a short while next week."

"I am afraid that I am going to the country," the Marquis replied. "You have made me neglect my duties to my estate and you know as well as I do that we must be very careful when your husband returns home."

The beauty pouted very prettily.

"You are making excuses," she said reproachfully, "but I want to see you and I so want to be with you."

The Marquis knew that this was true, but there was nothing he could do about it and he only hoped that she was not going to be difficult.

He invariably found that women made scenes when it came to bringing down the curtain on a love affair and he was never as distressed as the women were at having to go back to normality.

'Nothing can go on for ever,' he thought, 'and least of all a fiery passionate affair that has to be clandestine.'

The Count had watched what was happening with amusement.

"I guessed that there would be someone waiting for you as soon as you returned to London, Kelvin," he said. "You attract beautiful women and there is nothing you can do about it!"

The Marquis had never discussed his private affairs with anyone, not even the Count, and so he did not answer his somewhat mocking remarks.

Instead he asked,

"I am going to Queens Hoo tomorrow. Are you coming with me?"

"Of course. As you know, I have nothing particular to do at this moment and I always enjoy being at Queens Hoo more than anywhere else."

"I can say the same," the Marquis said, "I cannot imagine why I waste my time in London."

The Count laughed.

"That is certainly not the sort of way a Frenchman would describe it."

"But thank goodness I am not French. So I can be blunt and British!"

Both of them laughed and then they decided that they would drive down to Queens Hoo the next day rather than take the train.

"I suppose that you are still concentrating on your engine," the Count said.

"Of course," the Marquis answered. "And I am still trying to think of how I can avoid the difficulty you insist on confronting me with."

"I have told you how to do so, Kelvin."

"That is ridiculous," the Marquis said firmly. "Are you quite certain that there is no one else except this man, Galvani, who could build the engine for me?"

The Count made a gesture with his hand.

"There may be others, but I don't know of them. Galvani is undoubtedly the richest, the most interested and exactly the right man for the job."

"Apart from the conditions you think he will insist on making."

"Agreed! That is why you have to accept that my solution is the only possible one."

The Marquis said nothing and the Count went on,

"Quite frankly I would hate you to be disappointed. I really am convinced that he will lead you on by saying he will make the engine exactly to your design and then, when you think everything is settled, he produces his daughter."

"And you really still think that he will insist on my marrying her?"

"I am sure it will be a choice between having your engine and the daughter and starting all over again to find someone else to do what you require."

The Marquis was aware that that would be difficult.

He also knew that Italy was the country that would benefit greatly from a fully electrified railway system.

"We will think about it at Queens Hoo," the Count said. "Now stop looking worried. I want to be riding on one of your superlative horses instead of fretting about puffing train engines!"

The Marquis grinned.

"We will do that," he said, "so be round here about nine o'clock."

The Count was punctual and they set off.

The Marquis was driving his new team of perfectly matched chestnuts that the Count thought superb.

They drew an exceedingly smart chaise, which was black with yellow wheels and with the Marquis holding the reins every passer-by stopped to stare at them.

They stopped for luncheon at a Posting inn where the Marquis was known and, because Queens Hoo was not very far from London, they did not change horses.

After the rest the Marquis took them gently for the second part of the journey.

Because they had stayed rather longer than they had planned over luncheon, they did not arrive at Queens Hoo until nearly six o'clock.

One of the footmen saw them coming up the drive and he ran to tell Long, the butler, that his Lordship was approaching.

Almost as if they had been galvanised by electricity the whole house seemed to move into action.

And by the time the Marquis had driven his team into the courtyard outside the front door, the butler was in the hall with four footmen in attendance.

Mrs, Whicker was waiting at the top of the stairs in case his Lordship had brought an unexpected guest.

The Count was such a regular visitor that he had his own bedroom, which was seldom used by anyone else.

As the horses came to a standstill, the grooms came running to hold their heads and, as the Marquis stepped down, the Head Groom was waiting beside him.

"I have had an excellent journey, Groves," he said. "Give the horses a good rest tomorrow. They have carried us splendidly."

"I'll do that, my Lord," Groves said, touching his hat, "and it's glad we be to see your Lordship 'ome again."

"And I am always glad to be home," he answered.

He walked in at the front door and noticed with satisfaction the large bowl of flowers on the hall table.

There were flowers as well in the Queen's drawing room, which was a very lovely room.

As the Marquis expected there was an open bottle of champagne waiting in the gold ice-cooler which bore his Coat of Arms.

He and the Count had a drink and then the Marquis said,

"I suppose I had better look at the desk in my study and see if there are any urgent letters or messages for me. I always make Long keep them for a day after they arrive in case I turn up before he sends them to London."

"I know all your peculiarities," the Count said, "and I expect the first letter you open will be wet with tears!"

The Marquis knew he was referring to the beauty he had left behind him and so did not deign to answer.

He walked towards the study and the Count came out of the drawing room and went along the passage to where there was a door into the garden.

It was very much his Italian blood that made him find the garden at Queens Hoo so beautiful that it moved him emotionally.

It was by now after six o'clock and the sun was beginning to sink in the sky and birds were going to roost.

But there were still plenty of butterflies hovering over the flowers and the soft buzz of bees collecting pollen.

The Count walked slowly over the green grass that was as soft as velvet.

He went towards the shrubbery and the cascade and then, as he passed by the entrance to the Herb Garden, he thought that he would take a look at the fountain.

It always pleased his artistic sense to see the water flung up in the air and then in the sunshine it looked like little drops of the rainbow as it fell into the bowl beneath it.

He walked through the gate and then stopped.

He had expected the Herb Garden to be empty as it usually was.

To his surprise someone else was there.

He saw that it was a woman who seemed to be part of the falling water and the sunshine turned her hair to gold.

It was someone had never seen before.

She was, however, so lovely and so much part of the fountain that he felt that he was looking at a painting by some great Master.

Lola had no idea that he was there.

Tipping back her head, she was watching the water flying up into the sky then falling down onto the goldfish swimming beneath it.

She found herself entranced by the fountain every time she came to the Herb Garden.

She was also intending as soon as she had the time to ask Mrs. Whicker if she could make some of the herbal creams her mother had made.

One was a magical cure for anyone who had a cut or a bruise and another her mother was sure kept her skin so white and clear that she never had a line or a wrinkle.

The Count moved away and then he walked back to the house.

He found the Marquis coming back from his study and said to him,

"I would love another glass of champagne, Kelvin, and I also have a question to ask you."

The Marquis followed him into the drawing room.

"What is it?" he enquired.

"Why have you kept from me, your oldest friend, anything so exquisite and so exceptionally lovely?"

There was an accusing note in the Count's voice and the Marquis stared at him.

"What are you talking about?"

"Now come on, Kelvin, you know quite well what I am talking about and it is unlike you to have her at Queens Hoo."

He was aware that none of the Marquis's many love affairs had ever been conducted in his country home and it was as if he wished to keep the house sacred as it was where he had spent his childhood.

The Marquis, having poured the Count a glass of champagne, was helping himself to one.

"You are still talking gibberish, Camilo. What do I have here that you have not seen before?"

"That is the question I am asking you."

"As far as I know," the Marquis answered, "there is no one staying in the house except ourselves."

It passed through his mind that perhaps one of his relations had asked for a bed for the night thinking that he was away. It was unlikely and something he discouraged, but it could happen.

Then he thought, if that was so, Long would have told him as soon as he arrived.

The Count sipped his drink.

"You are either being very secretive, Kelvin," he said, "which I resent when it is applied to me or else I have had hallucinations."

"That is much more likely and, if you will tell me what you are talking about, I shall be able to understand."

"When you went to your study," the Count said, "I went into the garden, which is looking magnificent."

"Of course," the Marquis nodded.

"I thought I would take a look at the fountain in the Herb Garden," the Count went on. "There I saw standing beside it the most exquisite creature I have seen for years. Someone so lovely I could hardly believe that she is real."

"In which case she is not," the Marquis said. "As you have said yourself, you must be having hallucinations as there is no one like that at Queens Hoo."

"But I have just seen her with my own eyes," the Count insisted, "and I cannot help thinking, Kelvin, that you are either playing a trick on me or being extremely deceitful, which is something you never are."

"That is true," the Marquis said, "and, as far as I am concerned, you are talking sheer nonsense. But in case you are not, I am going to ring the bell and ask if anyone is staying here without my knowledge."

"I think that would spoil my story," the Count said, "come and see what I have seen for yourself."

"All right, Camilo, and, if there is nobody there, I think we should send for the doctor."

The Count paid no attention to that remark.

He drank a little more champagne, then put down his glass.

"Are you coming," he said, "or do you intend to tell me the truth."

"I think you have gone raving mad," the Marquis replied. "So I will come and see your ghost for myself. If it is a reality, I will then apologise for not informing you of what I did not know."

The Count did not want to spend any more time arguing and so he led the way to the door into the garden.

The two men walked across the lawn side by side until they came to the Herb Garden.

Then the Count, because he was impatient, walked a few paces ahead and passed through the gate.

To his disappointment there was no one there.

The fountain was still throwing its water up into the sky as he had seen before, but there was no evidence of the lovely creature with her golden hair catching the sun.

"She has gone!" he exclaimed.

"Then you *have* been seeing things," the Marquis said. "That will teach you not to drink too much."

"I had just the one glass of champagne," the Count protested. "I swear to you that she was here, looking up at the fountain and I have never seen anything so glorious."

"Well, there are supposed to be ghosts at Queens Hoo and one of my relations swore that he saw Queen Elizabeth herself. But personally I find it hard to believe in them and even harder to believe you."

"I saw her, I know I saw her," the Count insisted.

"Come back to the house. We will have everyone paraded in front of you and if you find anything exquisitely lovely in the kitchen staff or among the housemaids, who have been here for years, I will eat my hat!"

They walked back to the house almost in silence.

The Marquis appreciated the fact that the Count was still convinced in his own mind that he had seen this particular beauty who had moved him so deeply.

Secretly the Marquis thought it must be his friend's imagination, due, of course, to the mixed blood of two very romantic nations.

Hungarians and Italians, he now told himself, were always looking for love and they found it difficult not to be continually thinking about it.

'It starts when they are boys at school,' he thought.

It had never troubled him until he went to Oxford and before that he had been concerned with horse games and any kind of sport he could take part in.

'It is always the same with foreigners,' he reflected. 'With them it is always love, love, love, all the way from first thing in the morning until last thing at night.'

All he knew at this moment was that he was glad that his last love affair was over and, if he was honest, he knew that if it had gone on longer he would be bored.

When they entered the study, the Count then threw himself down into a comfortable chair.

"I saw her! I definitely saw her!"

"Have another glass of champagne," the Marquis said, "and you will doubtless see three of her, although two would be more convenient, one for you and one for me!"

The Count gave a short laugh.

"That would certainly 'be convenient', as you call it," he said, "but I am determined to find my enchantress however much you may scoff at me."

The Marquis threw up his arms.

"My house is yours and everything in it. Just help yourself and, if you wake up in the middle of the night and find that your enchantress is just some old woman, who is helping with the washing-up, don't blame me."

The Count finished his glass and rose to his feet.

"I am going to have a bath and, if there is a moon tonight, I shall go to the Herb Garden to see if my beautiful enchantress turns up again."

"Good luck and you have my blessing, Camilo."

The Marquis too finished his champagne and they walked up the stairs side by side.

The Count's room came first and he went into it to find his valet waiting for him.

The Marquis was just about to go on to the Master suite when Mrs. Whicker appeared.

"Good evening, my Lord," she said curtseying.

"Good evening, Mrs. Whicker," he replied, "I hope that you are well and there is no trouble in the house."

"None at all," she answered, "but I've somethin' to show your Lordship that I thinks will please you."

She was standing outside the Queen's bedroom and now she opened the door.

The Marquis knew immediately that he was to be shown the curtains that had worried him for so long and he doubted very much if they would please him now.

However, he realised that the candles were lit in the Queen's room and that the curtains were drawn.

"This is what I have to show your Lordship," Mrs. Wicker said, moving towards the nearest window.

It was the one, the Marquis was well aware, that was the worst damaged and he had almost despaired of it.

Three embroideresses had been dismissed as soon as he saw their work and he thought now that it was most unlikely since he had last been here at Queens Hoo that yet another had been in the least successful.

There was a large candelabrum holding six candles standing on the chest beside the window and it was easy to see in this light the beautiful pink velvet curtain with its flowers and leaves.

Automatically the Marquis's eyes went down to the ground where the curtain had been torn so badly and where the embroidery had been mended so abominably that it had to be unpicked.

Then, as he looked, he stopped and looked again.

Mrs. Whicker did not say anything, she was merely watching him as he bent down and picked up the edge of the curtain.

He stared at the embroidery that Lola had done and could not believe that it was the same curtain.

Without meaning to, he spoke his suspicion aloud,

"You have not changed this curtain for one of the others?"

"No, no, of course not, my Lord," Mrs. Whicker replied with a note of reproach in her voice.

"Then who has done such a splendid job?" he next asked. "I can hardly believe this is true after the ghastly failure of the last embroideress, it does not seem possible."

"That's exactly what I thought, my Lord,"

"Then how can you have found someone who can do it so well? It is brilliant, absolutely brilliant, and there is no other word for it."

"That's just what I said and I'm so glad that your Lordship thinks the same," Mrs. Whicker replied.

"Well, who is this genius and where did you find her?"

"She came down with me from London, my Lord, and I was ever so doubtful as to whether I should take her or not."

"Thank God you did," the Marquis exclaimed. "I was beginning to completely despair of ever making these curtains usable and now this one looks like new."

"Miss Fenton has only just started work on the next one," Mrs. Whicker said.

"Fenton," the Marquis repeated. "Is that her name? She must be very old to be so experienced. For goodness sake don't let her die until she has finished every curtain in the house!"

Mrs. Whicker laughed.

"She'll not be dyin', my Lord, for a long time."

A sudden idea came to the Marquis's mind.

"Are you saying the embroideress is young?"

"Yes, my Lord, she is very young, in fact it seems incredible that anyone could sew so brilliantly at the age of eighteen."

The Marquis was thinking of the Count's encounter in the Herb Garden.

"What is Miss Fenton like?" he asked.

"You'll see her for yourself," Mrs. Whicker replied, "and I think you'll be surprised."

The Marquis drew his watch from his pocket.

"Then I will see her now," he said. "I suppose she is staying in the house?"

"Yes, of course, my Lord. I'll go and tell her your Lordship wishes to meet her."

Mrs. Whicker hurried from the room and he stood gazing at the curtain that Lola had embroidered.

He could not believe it was the same curtain that had irritated him for so long.

He had been determined ever since he had inherited to make the house as perfect as he could and he wanted to ensure that it looked exactly as it had when it was first built for Queen Elizabeth.

The curtains had survived because the velvet was so thick and of the finest quality and the lining had, he was sure, fallen into tatters many times as the centuries passed.

The whole room was now as it had looked in the days of the Virgin Queen and there were endless notes in the diaries of the time of her at Queens Hoo.

The days she spent hunting in the woods and later in the year shooting wild stags with a crossbow were all recorded in detail.

The Marquis had, when he was quite young, read and re-read these reports and he had liked to imagine the Queen, still young and beautiful, enjoying the comfort and charm of her bedroom.

He had gone to a great deal of trouble to find men who could repair the carvings on the bed and the pelmets over the windows.

Now, with the exception of the curtains, he thought the Queen might, if she came back, find it as satisfactory as she had when she was on the throne. He had imagined her sitting by the mirror on her dressing table surrounded by carved golden angels.

The carpet had actually become threadbare and in such a bad state it could not be repaired and at enormous expense the Marquis had arranged for it to be copied by Persian carpet makers.

It was now the same design and colour as when it was first made for the Queen.

He had said to himself only a little while ago that the room was perfect except for the curtains and one failure after another had made him begin to despair of completing the restoration.

Now, when he had almost given up hope, a magic wand had been waved and the room had now begun to look exactly as he had hoped it would.

He was well aware that there was a great deal to be done to the other curtains, especially those on the bed, but there would be no difficulty now.

By a miracle they had found an embroideress who could make good the disaster the last person had created and repair the damage that had hurt the Marquis every time he looked at it.

He was again holding the curtain in his hands and looking at the tiny little stitches that created the flowers.

They and the leaves were so well done that they almost seemed to be living.

Then he heard the door open behind him.

He thought that it would be Mrs. Whicker bringing the embroideress.

He turned round and there was only one person standing inside the door.

And he knew at once that he was gazing at the girl the Count had described as being exquisite!

She was looking at him, he realised, enquiringly and there was also a look of astonishment in her eyes.

Before he could say anything, she blurted out as if she could not help herself,

"Oh, I thought you would be very old!"

CHAPTER FOUR

Lola realised she had spoken her thoughts aloud.

"I am sorry," she said quickly before the Marquis could say anything. "I am so very sorry."

"Why should you expect me to be old?" he asked curiously.

She walked across the room towards him, fearing that she had made a major gaffe.

She was wondering what she should do about it.

Realising that he was waiting for her answer as she stood beside him, she said a little hesitatingly,

"It is because you always expect perfection and, as you have done so much to the house, I thought it must have taken you many years."

The Marquis smiled.

"A good explanation, but I am surprised that no one informed you that I am still considered a young man."

"I suppose they took it for granted," Lola replied, "and they do all they can to make the house as perfect as you want it to be."

"What do you think of Queens Hoo?" he enquired.

"I think it is the most beautiful Elizabethan house I have ever seen," Lola replied, "and, as I have always lived in one myself, I find everything about it wonderful."

"You have lived in an Elizabethan house yourself?"

There was no doubt that the Marquis was surprised and then, before Lola could answer, he said,

"Perhaps that is why you can embroider so well and I can only say to you, Miss Fenton, that as well as being astonished I am delighted with what you have done so far."

"Mrs. Whicker was very worried that you would be disappointed," Lola said.

The Marquis was now looking down at the curtain that she had mended.

"I find it difficult to understand," he said, "how you can do such exquisite embroidery when you are so young. If you are surprised that I am not old, I too was expecting someone with vast experience and who would have taken at least forty years to acquire the art of embroidery."

Lola grinned.

"Well, I am not as old as that yet and I am so glad that you are pleased with what I have done already."

"I am indeed pleased. It is exactly what I wanted, but thought I would never be able to see it."

"It is a very beautiful pattern and you are lucky, since the curtains are so old, that the damage is not worse."

"It is bad enough, but, seeing what you have done, I really believe that this room will be exactly as it was when Queen Elizabeth stayed here."

"I can imagine her wandering about in such a very beautiful place," Lola said, "to escape from all the pomp and circumstance she had to endure in London."

"I often thought about that when I was a boy," the Marquis agreed. "Of course you realise, Miss Fenton, that this is not the only room in the house, which needs your magical work to bring it back to what it was originally."

"I have not really had time to look at the curtains in the other rooms, but I cannot believe that they would be more difficult than these."

"I was not thinking of the difficulty," the Marquis said, "but that you may have other engagements waiting and therefore you cannot stay long at Queens Hoo."

"I can stay as long as you would want me – "

She spoke eagerly and the Marquis looked at her, she thought, with surprise.

"What about your parents? What would they have to say to that?" he asked.

Lola realised that Mrs. Whicker had not told him anything about her and she thought that it was because the housekeeper wanted to give the Marquis a surprise.

She must have known that he would be expecting someone very much older and she had gathered from the way Mrs. Whicker had talked about them that the previous embroideresses had not only been middle-aged but dull and exceedingly plain.

Now she replied quickly,

"My father and mother are both dead and I am an orphan. To be truthful I thought that I was very lucky to obtain this position when I applied for work at Mrs. Hill's Agency in Mount Street."

"And I should have thought that you were much too young to have to look for work from an Agency. Surely you have relatives who would let you stay with them?"

He was thinking of how easily she might have gone to a place where men would shock and frighten her.

There was no doubt that the Count had been right when he claimed that she was very lovely.

The more the Marquis looked at her the more he became convinced that she was without exception the most beautiful young woman he had ever seen.

He saw that her beauty was enhanced by the fact that she was so young and obviously very unsophisticated.

She was a lady, there was no doubt about that.

How was it possible that a lady could be wandering about London alone trying to find employment?

If there was one thing the Marquis enjoyed, it was a mystery and, as he was talking to Lola, he found himself speculating about her and he wanted to find out more.

Was it possible that she was not an orphan but had run away from home? Was there perhaps a more sinister reason, such as having to marry a man she hated?

He found these questions buzzing in his brain and he knew that he would have to seek out the truth.

To prolong the interview and, having examined the curtains in the Queen's Room, he took her into one of the State rooms on the opposite side of the corridor.

Here the curtains were green and embroidered with birds and butterflies and some were sadly faded and, on her inspection of the rooms with Mrs. Whicker, Lola had not realised how pretty these particular curtains were.

"I shall enjoy doing these!" she exclaimed. "I have done butterflies before, but not so many birds."

"Do you think you can manage them?" he asked.

"Of course I can!"

She touched one of the curtains very gently with the tips of her fingers as she said,

"How lucky the Queen was to have so many people in those days who could embroider so skilfully. And you would think that we would be able to do better today, but instead we just have to copy what they have done first."

"I have often thought," the Marquis replied, "that we have so much to learn from the Elizabethans."

"Of course you are right!" Lola exclaimed. "I am longing to spend time in your Picture Gallery, but I had to work very hard so as to have something to show you when you arrived home."

The Marquis smiled.

"You are making me out a real bogey or should it be an ogre?"

"I hope that you are neither, but I was frightened that you would not be satisfied with what I had done and show me the door."

"What would you have done if I had?"

"I think I would have sat down and cried and rather than leave this lovely place, drowned myself in the lake."

"You know quite well you would not have done so, but I am interested to know where you would have gone."

Lola thought of her uncle and gave a little shiver.

"Somewhere where I would have been extremely unhappy," she said, "which for the moment, thanks to Mrs. Whicker and, of course, you, I can avoid."

The Marquis longed to ask her more, but he felt it would be a mistake on so short an acquaintance.

"I must now go and dress for dinner," he said. "In the meantime thank you, Miss Fenton, for the magnificent start you have made on my curtains. I shall look forward to seeing them all looking as they did when they were first hung for the Queen."

"I can only hope you will not be disappointed."

The Marquis went from the room and, as he walked to his Master suite, he thought that here was a puzzle that he had to solve.

'Just how is it possible that anyone so young and so beautiful can embroider so well?' he asked himself. 'And who is she to be wandering around with no parents and no Guardian?'

As he went into his room, he was thinking that Lola had spoken to him almost as if she was an equal.

He was quite sure that it had never struck her for a moment that she should have curtseyed and addressed him continually as 'my Lord'.

'Who is she?' he asked himself. 'How is it possible that she has come here to Queens Hoo instead of wasting her talents on someone who would not appreciate them?'

When he went downstairs to dinner a little late, the Count was waiting for him and he began,

"I have solved the problem, Camilo. You were not hallucinating or seeing ghosts. You were seeing a new member of my household, an embroideress who is working on the Queen's curtains."

The Count stared at him.

"Are you telling me that that exquisite creature is one of your staff?"

"I can hardly believe it myself and, as it is a puzzle, I want your help in trying to solve it."

"If it means meeting the lovely, sylph-like Goddess I saw staring into the fountain, the sooner the better," the Count replied. "Why did you not ask her to dine with us?"

"I can hardly do that when I am employing her and I suppose she eats in the housekeeper's room."

"How could you possibly treat her in such a way?" the Count demanded. "And, what is more important, when can I meet her?"

Before the Marquis could reply, Long announced dinner and they walked towards the dining room.

They were both aware that it would be a mistake to talk about Lola in front of the other servants and so they talked on other subjects until the meal was finished.

As they left the dining room, the Count asked,

"Have you been thinking over what you will now do about Galvani? If you are not going to Italy, I will have to let him know that you have changed your mind."

"Changed my mind? Why should I do that?"

"I thought when you left London, Kelvin, that you were determined not to take my advice, in which case the whole trip will be wasted."

The Marquis did not reply and the Count went on,

"Incidentally I have spent a great deal of my time on you. I did not want to go to Florence to find Galvani and I stayed there four days and nights convincing him of the brilliance of your invention."

"I would suppose there must be others who could manufacture my engine," the Marquis said reflectively.

"I can think of no one at the moment," the Count replied. "As you know, most railway systems either have some expert of their own who would resent any rivalry or else they would look to existing organisations in America and England to satisfy their immediate requirements."

Then, as the Count sipped his brandy, he said,

"For goodness sake don't let's start talking about your electric engine. I am so much more interested at the moment in this entrancing young woman you have hidden away and whom you pretend you have never seen before."

"I promise you that is the truth," the Marquis said, "and, as she is very young and, I am certain, innocent, I think the less she sees of you the better!"

"So you want to keep her for yourself."

"It is nothing like that," the Marquis insisted. "I have been completely honest with you, Camilo. I had not seen her or known of her existence until today."

"Then why are you making such a fuss about her? Or are you perhaps a dog in the manger?"

"Oh, very well," the Marquis said, "as you are so curious, I will send for her."

He put out his hand towards the bell-pull and there was silence until the door opened.

"We would like, Long," the Marquis said, "to talk to Miss Fenton about her embroidery."

"Miss Fenton's retired to bed, my Lord," the butler replied. "Mrs. Whicker arranged that she has supper in her bedroom and the housemaid has informed me that after her tray's been taken away, she gets into bed and reads."

"In which case, of course, you cannot disturb her. Thank you, Long, that will be all."

"What do you make of it?" the Count asked. "Why should she have supper in her bedroom?"

"I know the answer. As she is my housekeeper's protégée and, since Mrs. Whicker is as aware as I am that she is a lady, she does not eat with the other staff."

"It seems to me very odd, Kelvin, but then English customs are always incomprehensible!"

The Marquis said nothing, he suddenly thought that he had no wish to go on taking about his mysterious new employee, but would work out the puzzle for himself.

She was at the moment not overawed by him or the house as he might have expected and therefore it would be a mistake to upset her or make her nervous in any way.

He had not, however, taken into consideration the Count's interest in her.

*

They went out riding early the next morning before breakfast, which was always the Marquis's favourite time.

"I don't mind betting you quite a large sum," the Count said, "that, as your hidden Goddess is so beautiful and also English, she can ride as well as sew."

The Marquis looked at him in surprise.

"Are you suggesting that I should mount her?"

"I was just thinking how elegant she would look on one of your finest horses. I have never argued against your contention that English women ride far better than those of any other nation!"

His eyes were twinkling as he went on,

"Therefore I would like to see someone so exquisite on the black stallion you are riding or perhaps on that grey horse you call Snowball."

The Marquis thought that it would certainly make a pretty picture, yet he did not want to encourage the Count's interest in someone who was so essential to him.

It was only as they cantered back for breakfast that they saw her.

Lola had risen early.

She wanted plenty of time to walk in the garden before she went into the Queen's bedroom to continue her work on the curtains.

She had been first to the fountain and then went to the cascade. Because she was curious she had followed it down through the trees until it reached the stream.

When she arrived there, she saw to her delight that there were a clutch of newly hatched ducklings swimming around their mother.

The swans had also produced a family and nothing could be prettier than the mother swimming proudly down the lake with her babies following her.

It was, of course, the Count who saw her as they crossed the bridge.

Instead of riding towards the courtyard, he turned his horse onto the grass and trotted towards Lola and there was nothing the Marquis could do but follow him.

The Count reached her first and, sweeping off his hat, he began,

"Good morning, Miss Fenton. I have heard his Lordship singing your praises and feel I must add mine."

Lola smiled.

"I suppose you are talking about the curtains in the Queen's room."

"Of course," the Count replied.

He dismounted and Lola moved to pat his horse.

As she did so, the Marquis joined them.

"Good morning, Miss Fenton," he said. "Are you studying the ducks and swans so that you can incorporate them with the other birds that we looked at last night?"

"I think you are suggesting indirectly that I ought to be working. I am just allowing myself a short walk in your wonderful garden before I pick up my needle."

"He is a slave-driver," the Count said. "Of course you must have time to see his Lordship's gardens, which are famous and his lake which I find very beautiful."

"So do I," Lola replied, "but I don't think anything could be more majestic that these two horses."

She moved towards the Marquis as she spoke. It was a very fine stallion that he was riding, jet-black with a single white mark on his nose.

"They are two of the finest horses that I have ever seen," she said almost as if she was speaking to herself.

"You are interested in horses?" the Marquis asked. "I suppose that means you have lived in the country."

"Yes, I have never been to London until I went to the Domestic Agency. I love horses even though we could afford only one."

She was thinking of how she had ridden her father's horse whenever she had the chance and hunted on him.

"If you want to ride, Miss Fenton," the Marquis said after a moment's pause, "I am sure my Head Groom will manage to find a horse you can handle."

"It's not a case of not being able to handle a horse," Lola replied a little indignantly, "but of having one at all."

"My stable is full," the Marquis smiled.

"Oh thank you! Thank you. It is something I enjoy more than anything else and I promise that I will not let it interfere with my work."

She thought for a moment and then she added,

"I will get up very early and ride before I have had breakfast. Then you cannot think I am defrauding you."

The Count laughed.

"You cannot quarrel with that, Kelvin."

"I was not thinking of quarrelling. I just want Miss Fenton to enjoy herself here so that she does not find it so dull that she wishes to leave me."

"You need not worry about that," Lola said. "I find Queens Hoo very exciting and I think it will take me ages to see everything here and how clever you have been."

The Count looked at the Marquis with a twinkle in his eyes and then, to both men's surprise, Lola said,

"Now I must go to work or you will think that I am wasting my time. Thank you for saying that I may ride, it is something very thrilling for me to look forward to."

She was moving as she said the last words and then she started to run.

She moved with a grace that the Marquis thought he had never seen in any other woman. Far sooner than he thought possible she had reached the courtyard and then disappeared through the front door.

The Count drew in his breath.

"You just never cease to surprise me, Kelvin. How, when you have everything in the world that you have ever wanted, you could manage to acquire anything so perfect as that young Goddess, I don't know."

"She is certainly original in what she says and what she does," the Marquis admitted. "I cannot help thinking that she is hiding from someone who sooner or later will turn up and claim her."

"It's a possibility," the Count agreed.

Then, as he mounted his horse, he said suddenly,

"But, of course, she has come to serve you, not only as regards your curtains but also your electric engine."

"What are you saying?" the Marquis enquired.

"Like a gift directly from the Gods, that beautiful girl has been sent to you so that you will have no problems with Galvani."

The Marquis stared at his friend.

"Are you now seriously suggesting that I ask Miss Fenton to go with me to Italy?"

"Why not?" the Count replied. "I would take her myself if I had the chance."

"You are not to dare to take her away from me until she has finished my curtains," the Marquis said quickly.

"At least I will wait until you have returned from Italy. I cannot interfere with a solution to your problem so miraculous that it must have come from Heaven itself."

"How could I ask a girl of that age to go with me in disguise to deceive an Italian railway magnate, Camilo?"

"Very easily, if you pay her. She has to earn her living and, if you pay her a decent sum for acting as your wife for the short time you will spend with Galvani, who is to know and who, for that matter, would care?"

"Galvani will be well aware, if he has ever been in England or reads the newspapers, that I am not married," the Marquis countered sharply.

"Galvani is very Italian and is not the slightest bit interested in what happens elsewhere. The Continent is his playground and he has no desire to go any further."

The Marquis smiled, but did not interrupt.

"What he really does want is a prestigious title for his daughter and I think he realises that he is not going to get it in Italy and he would therefore accept as second best a son-in-law who is an English Marquis."

"That is something he will not get from me!"

"Then the solution has dropped down like Manna from Heaven," the Count said. "Ask that lovely creature if she will go with you to Italy and I am quite certain that, like every other woman you have ever met, Kelvin, she will jump at the opportunity of being with you."

The Marquis did not speak until they were outside the front door and the grooms were hurrying towards them.

Then he said,

"I will think over all that you have just suggested, Camilo, but I have a feeling that the answer I shall get from my consideration will be a definite 'no'."

The Count, however, was not to be silenced.

"Nothing ventured, nothing win," he intoned.

Then, as the Marquis joined him and they walked up the steps, he added in a low voice,

"A faint heart never won anything and that is an undeniable fact."

The Marquis had a great number of letters waiting for his attention and, when breakfast was finished, he went to his study and his secretary joined him.

So the Count thought that he would go and see Lola as he wanted to inspect the problem curtains for himself.

He went up the stairs and found her, as he expected, in the Queen's room.

The sunshine coming through the bow window was shining on her hair and he saw with the pink of the curtains beside her that she made a very lovely picture.

As he walked across the room, Lola turned her head and, when she saw who it was, she smiled.

"Have you come to see that I am not wasting my time?" she asked. "Look!"

She held up the end of the second curtain she was working on that was on the other side of the window from the one she had finished.

She had already washed it and, although it was not torn, the embroidery had been somewhat damaged in one way or another and she had to remove what was left of it.

As the Count came to her side, she suggested,

"If you want to see what I have done, look at the curtain on the other side of the window."

She pointed towards it and he exclaimed,

"Now I know that they were not exaggerating when they said you are brilliant."

"Thank you," Lola said. "I have never had so many compliments in such a short time and I am feeling quite dizzy with them."

"Then you will have a great many more, not only as regards your work but because you yourself look like a piece of exquisite embroidery."

Lola did not look shy, but merely laughed.

"Which am I more like? The nice fat little bird just above my head or the pink flowers, which I shall have to copy until it is not surprising if I do look like one?"

"You look like yourself," the Count said, "and no one could ask for more."

She gave a little chuckle and went on sewing.

"Why are you laughing at what I said?" the Count enquired. "I mean it in all sincerity."

"I am sure you did. My father always told me that the French and Italians pay the most fulsome compliments, but they don't really mean as much as an Englishman when he says, 'you look all right, my dear'!"

She imitated her father's voice when she said the last words and now it was the Count who was laughing.

"That is not the right way to take a compliment."

"What is the right way?" Lola enquired of him.

"At your tender age you should look shy and flutter your eyelashes and murmur that you have never thought of yourself like that."

Now Lola laughed again.

"Is that what Italian men want?" she asked. "I am sure any Englishman would think it very silly."

"If he paid you a compliment, which is unlikely, he would expect you to appreciate it and to be overcome by his generosity in paying it."

"Now I think you are being rather sarcastic," Lola retorted, "and perhaps unkind to Englishmen."

As she said the last words, the door opened and the Marquis came in.

The Count was aware as he walked across the room towards them that he was annoyed at finding him there.

"Oh, here you are, Camilo," he began. "I wondered what had happened to you."

"I came to praise Miss Fenton for the miraculous way she has transformed your curtains. You have groaned about them for so long, but now you can never complain about them again."

"I am aware of that," the Marquis said. "I only hope, Miss Fenton, that my friend has not been interfering with your work."

"He was making me laugh," Lola replied, "but, as you can see, I am still stitching away."

She had looked up when the Marquis appeared and now her head was bent over her work and he could only see the top of her golden hair.

"I think," the Marquis said to the Count, "we must not interrupt Miss Fenton. I have so much for her to do that it makes me feel embarrassed if we delay her."

The Count looked at the Marquis and he knew that his friend was mocking him.

"But, of course. I know when I am not wanted."

The Count walked across the room without saying anything more and closed the door behind him.

For a second the Marquis thought of following him and then, as if he felt compelled to do what the Count had suggested, he said,

"I want to speak to you, Miss Fenton, and perhaps this is a good opportunity."

She looked up quickly and there was an expression in her eyes that he did not understand.

"You are not satisfied with me? You want me to leave?"

"No, of course not. I can assure you that you are completely indispensable. I have never found anyone who can embroider as well as you."

He saw Lola give a little sigh of relief and then he sat down on the stool in front of the dressing table.

"I have a proposition to make to you which would be of enormous help to me, but I shall quite understand if you refuse to do what I ask."

"What is it you want?" Lola asked.

She was puzzled, thinking that this was something that she had not expected.

"It is a secret from all except my closest friends," the Marquis confided, "but I have always been interested, one might say obsessed, by railway engines."

Lola's eyes widened.

"Railway engines!" she exclaimed.

"It may seem odd to you since, as you know, I love my beautiful house and everything that is Elizabethan. At the same time I find myself, almost as if I am compelled to do so, designing railway trains."

"How exciting for you! I have never thought of it before, but I can understand, because they are so new and very different from horses, that they have an interest all of their own."

The Marquis thought that no other woman he had ever met could be so understanding.

He went on to tell Lola how long it had taken him to design his electric engine and how much he wanted to see it in operation and she enthused,

"But of course you do and I think it very clever of you to do anything so difficult and so very up to date and exactly what is intriguing the whole world."

She had read with her father quite a lot about the railways that had been built in America and England and also read about rail developments in European countries.

There was no doubt that England was the pioneer as far as Europe was concerned and she thought it typical that men like the Marquis should be so interested.

"You will understand," he was now saying, "that I cannot build this engine myself for the simple reason that, if I had any connection with the business of railways, it would surprise and deeply shock my family."

"They will have to move with the times eventually. Papa said railways were being developed everywhere and in a few years everyone would travel by them instead of by road because they were so much quicker."

"Your father was so right," the Marquis said, "but I cannot become involved with any railway in England. I therefore want to have my engine made secretly in another country and no one here must know anything about it."

"It sounds rather sad that you will get no credit for being so clever, but I suppose people would be shocked at you being in trade," Lola commented.

He was surprised that she had used almost the same phrase he had used himself and that she should understand why it was wrong for him.

He continued, getting rather slowly, he was aware, to the whole point of the story,

"My friend, the Count, has recently returned from Italy. He has found a very rich man who is quite prepared to build my engine and use it where electric trains would be especially effective in that mountainous country."

"Yes, of course, I can understand that," Lola said, "and I did read somewhere that the steam locomotives they are using at the moment are not good on steep gradients or in tunnels."

The Marquis stared at her.

"Where did you read that?"

"It must have been in one of the newspapers," Lola replied. "Please go on."

"The man the Count has found for me is ready to go ahead but, and I am being very frank and confidential with you on this, Miss Fenton, he has a daughter for whom he is determined to obtain a title."

Lola's eyes widened.

"So he will want you to marry his daughter?" she exclaimed.

"Exactly. The Count is absolutely certain that, if I refuse to do so, he will refuse to build my engine."

"It really amounts to blackmail!" Lola cried.

The Marquis though it extremely intelligent of her to grasp the whole situation so clearly.

"I have been wondering," he said, "what I could do. The Count has suggested that I should take someone with me who acts the part of being my wife."

"You don't think that the Italian would find out?"

"The Count thinks it most unlikely especially if I say I married quietly because my wife is in mourning."

As he said the last words, it suddenly struck Lola why he was telling her this.

She looked at him in astonishment.

Then she said,

"You are not suggesting – you are not saying this to me because – "

"I am asking you to be brave and adventurous," the Marquis said quietly, "and to travel with me to Italy just while I complete my negotiations with the Italian."

He paused and then went on,

"It should not take more than three weeks, perhaps less and I am prepared to pay you one thousand pounds for helping me out of a very difficult dilemma."

Lola gasped.

It had flashed instantly through her mind, when she had thought incredulously that the Marquis was asking her to go with him, that she must refuse.

It was something that both her father and mother would disapprove of.

But one thousand pounds!

She could hardly believe that she had heard right.

Then she knew at once that, if she had one thousand pounds, there would be no need for her ever to go to live with her Uncle Arthur.

She would be able to pay for a chaperone and she could then go back to her adored Meadow Cottage when she had finished her work at Queens Hoo.

And she would not have any worries over money for a very long time.

"I cannot tell just you how grateful I would be," the Marquis was saying, "if you will do this. Although it is a long way to travel, I think you will find it enjoyable and we will do it in the most comfortable way possible."

There was silence for a moment and then Lola said,

"Did you really say that you would give me one thousand pounds?"

"It is a small way to express my gratitude for what you would be doing for me."

As he spoke, he rose from the stool.

"You don't have to decide at once," he said, "I have only just returned from Germany and I want to stay here and relax a little. But then I cannot wait too long."

He walked towards the door and, when he reached it, he hesitated for a moment and turned back.

"By the way, Miss Fenton, while you are thinking about it, I suggest that you ride tomorrow morning before breakfast with my friend and myself. You can choose any horse you like from my stables."

He did not wait for her reply, but opened the door and went out onto the landing.

He was intelligent enough to guess that what he had offered her for tomorrow morning was even more tempting than the one thousand pounds that she obviously needed.

'Camilo was right,' he thought, 'it would be a great mistake for me to be involved with some Italian girl whom I have no intention of marrying and at least that problem will not occur where Miss Fenton is concerned.'

He reflected as he walked down the stairs that he would have to be astute and make sure that the staff did not realise why he was taking her away.

However, it should not be beyond his imagination to concoct a story that she had to go away for a few weeks, perhaps to look after a sick relative before she returned to finish the curtains.

He was determined that nothing and nobody should prevent him from keeping Lola as his embroideress.

'By this time next year the house will look perfect,' he told himself as he walked across the hall.

And by then his electric train would be running in Italy.

'Camilo is quite right,' he thought as he opened the drawing room door, 'Miss Fenton has dropped down like a gift from the Gods.'

CHAPTER FIVE

It seemed to Lola that she was in a dream.

Ever since she had made up her mind to accept the Marquis's invitation to travel with him to Italy, things had happened very quickly.

She had not told him that she would do so until after they had been riding the following morning.

She fortunately had in her trunk her mother's riding habit, which was far smarter than her own and, as she well knew, it was more suitable for someone grown up.

When she appeared at the stables, she thought that both the Marquis and the Count looked at her admiringly.

She was, however, much more concerned with the horses than with them, as the Marquis had told her that she could ride whichever one she liked.

She went from stall to stall, thinking that each one was more magnificent than the last.

Finally, after the Count had suggested it, she chose the white horse called Snowball.

"When I first saw you," he said, "I knew I wanted to see you riding a white horse."

Lola looked at him in surprise, thinking that until they had so recently been introduced they had never met.

"I saw you at the fountain in the Herb Garden," he explained, "but afterwards I thought that you must be just an illusion since no one could look lovelier."

Lola stared at him thinking that she could not have heard him aright.

Then, when she saw the expression in his eyes, she blushed.

And it made her look, the Count was thinking, even more exquisite.

The Marquis, who had not heard this conversation as he was talking to the Head Groom, joined them.

"Have you made up your mind, Miss Fenton?" he asked.

"I should like to ride Snowball," she replied.

The names of the horses in the stables were printed over their mangers. It was something that Lola had not seen before and she thought it an excellent idea.

"I very much approve of your choice," the Marquis said, "because Snowball is very well trained and so I can thoroughly recommend him."

"I am sure that applies to every one of your horses," she said, "and I only wish that my mother and father could see them."

"Did they ride as well as I am sure you do?" the Count asked.

"My mother was greatly admired when she hunted with the Combe," Lola replied.

The Count looked surprised.

He was naturally thinking it somewhat strange, if Miss Fenton's mother could hunt, that she was obliged to earn her living.

Meanwhile the Marquis, who had been speaking to the groom about a side-saddle, came back to the stall.

"Now Miss Fenton has made her choice," he said, "let's get going. Otherwise it will have to be a short ride and I need a long one."

He went out into the yard as he spoke and mounted the black stallion, which was one of his favourites, while the Count rode another fine stallion that was very nearly as outstanding.

As soon as Lola was in the saddle, they started off.

She could not help thinking that the Marquis would not expect her to be a good rider if she was so poor and so she galloped a little faster and they had to urge their horses to keep up with her.

At the end of the flat ground there was a fence and, as it appeared a little way ahead of them, the Marquis said,

"There is no need for you to jump the fence which is just ahead, Miss Fenton. There is a gate to the left of it."

Lola pretended not to hear him.

She took the fence in style and was followed by both the Marquis and the Count.

When they reached the other side, the Count said,

"I was right, I knew I would be. You ride exactly as I expected."

Lola smiled at him.

Then she was aware that for some reason that she did not understand the Marquis was frowning.

Actually he was thinking that it was a mistake for the Count to make so much fuss of someone who was in his employment. It might turn her head so that she would have ideas 'above her station'.

He therefore deliberately prevented there being any further conversation by setting a fast pace and, when they turned round to go back to the house for breakfast, it was after eight-thirty.

As soon as they had taken the horses to the stables, the Marquis then hurried the Count into the house, making no suggestion that Lola should go with them.

It was only what she expected and so she therefore deliberately spent a little time stroking Snowball and, when the two men were out of sight, she went into the house by a back entrance.

She thought with delight as she went upstairs that now she had been allowed to ride the Marquis's horses it would be difficult for him to refuse to allow her to do so again, especially if he was away from Queens Hoo.

Then she remembered that she had to decide if she would go to Italy with him.

'One thousand pounds!' she said to herself again. 'It will mean I never have to worry about having to live with Uncle Arthur.'

She was working it out in her mind.

After she was paid for her work on the Marquis's curtains she would have an additional one thousand pounds in the bank and then she could go back to Meadow Cottage or find another position where she could embroider.

She would have a reference from the Marquis and it would be a glowing one and ancestral houses with ancient curtains would be delighted to employ her.

The whole idea made her so happy that she wanted to jump for joy.

'I am lucky, just incredibly lucky,' she thought as she changed from her riding clothes, 'and, of course, I must do what the Marquis wants.'

When, after her breakfast, she went to the Queen's room, she felt that he would come to hear her decision.

She was not mistaken.

She had been working for an hour when he came in.

"I thought I would find you here," he began.

"I am working very hard and very quickly," Lola replied, "and thank you so much for that wonderful ride this morning. It is something I shall always remember."

"I hope you will have a great number of other rides to remember. And I am really wondering if you are brave enough to ride in a train as far as Florence – "

There was a touch of humour in his voice, but Lola was, however, aware that he was anxious for her to give him the answer he desired.

She smiled and then she said,

"If you are quite certain that no one will ever know that I was acting a part in pretending to be your wife and, if it will really help you, then, of course, I must say 'yes'."

"You will do it!" the Marquis exclaimed. "I am very grateful."

Lola was looking at him enquiringly and he added,

"I will take every precaution to ensure that no one is aware of what we are doing, except, of course, the Count who has arranged it for me."

"And he will not talk?" Lola questioned.

"He is a diplomat," the Marquis replied, "and they are trained from the moment they enter the Service to be extremely discreet."

Lola gave a sigh of relief, as she was afraid that in some unfortunate way her uncle might hear about what she was doing and she was well aware how shocked and angry he would be.

"Then what are we going to do?" she asked a little helplessly.

"I have it all planned," the Marquis said, lowering his voice. "You will receive a letter tomorrow, which will inform you that one of your relatives is very ill and it is absolutely essential you should see her before she dies."

He thought for a moment before he went on,

"You will hint to me you expect that she has left you something in her will and anyway you could not be so unkind as to not go to her when she is asking for you."

Lola nodded.

"I will then say that, as I am going to London," the Marquis continued, "and, as it would be a mistake for you, being so young, to travel alone, you had better travel with me. In London you will go to the Count's house while I get you a passport. I presume you don't have one?"

"No, of course not."

"Then as soon as I have arranged it, we will leave immediately for Dover."

"You make it sound so easy," Lola told him. "At the same time, although I am very excited at the idea, I do hope that no one will find out."

"I am certain that you will be quite safe and I just cannot believe that we shall be unfortunate enough to meet any acquaintances on the train."

He thought that it was rather presumptuous of Miss Fenton to imagine that she would be recognised.

She would be travelling First Class and with every possible luxury and if by chance she had any friends on the train, they would doubtless be in a Second Class carriage, and eating in the station buffets, which he never did.

However, he was very grateful that she would play the part and he merely said,

"Leave everything to me. Just look upset when you receive the letter that I have written to you."

Lola smiled.

"I will do so, but you know that Mrs. Whicker will be very curious and anxious about the curtains."

"All you have to do is to assure her that you will be returning here as soon as possible. She knows better than anyone else how much I want the curtains finished."

"I promise I will come back and finish them."

"You know as far as Queens Hoo is concerned," the Marquis said, "that you are indispensable."

He left the Queen's room and Lola was wondering if his plan would really be successful.

*

She received the letter the next morning through the post and the Marquis had indeed written a sad letter telling her about her aunt's illness and how they thought that she could not survive.

She realised that he was afraid that she might leave the letter lying about and this, she told herself somewhat indignantly, she would not have done.

At the same time it reassured her that the Marquis was being careful about every detail.

As she expected, when she told Mrs. Whicker that she had to leave, the housekeeper was almost hysterical.

"You can't go now!" she exclaimed. "You haven't finished the curtains."

"I will come back the moment my aunt either dies or gets better," Lola replied, "and, as she is very old, I am afraid that she will probably die."

"But surely there are other people to look after her beside you?" Mrs. Whicker quizzed her.

"Not many and she has always been very fond of me and promised me certain things in her will."

As she had always hated lying, she said as little as possible while Mrs. Whicker kept pleading with her.

Finally, when she heard that the Marquis was going to escort Lola to London, she ceased trying to prevent her from leaving.

She only made her promise again that she would return as quickly as possible.

"If there's any question of your aunt lingerin' for weeks or perhaps months," she said, "you must come back. You knows as well as I does that his Lordship'll never be satisfied until all them curtains are finished."

"I will definitely come back," Lola promised.

Then, almost before she had time to say any more, the clothes she wanted to take with her were packed.

She drove to the station in the same carriage as the Marquis and the Count and she sat with them in a reserved compartment after the Express had stopped at the Halt.

In London Lola found the Count's house far more attractive than the hostility of Kencombe House.

After the Marquis had procured her passport from the Foreign Office, they sat down to a delicious meal that Lola learnt was cooked by a French chef.

"I know he should be Italian," the Count said, "but, while you will find the food in Florence enjoyable, there is no one in the world who can cook as well as the French."

"That is what I have always heard," Lola said, "and while I will appreciate the food, what I really want is to see the Art Galleries while I am in Florence and, of course, the Ponte Vecchio."

"I doubt if his Lordship will even notice the Ponte Vecchio or anything else in Florence," the Count pointed out. "It will be engines, engines, engines all the time!"

"Now you are just being insulting," the Marquis said. "If you like, I will promise Miss Fenton that she is to see at least some of the beauty of Florence even while I am thinking how quickly my engine will comb the Apennines and travel through the dark tunnels."

"So there you are!" the Count said to Lola. "And when you return, you will be so glad to see Snowball and all the other horses that you will never want to hear the wheels of a train again!"

She knew that he was only teasing the Marquis and therefore she did not answer.

But the Marquis burst out,

"Oh, for goodness sake, Camilo, stop frightening Miss Fenton! Otherwise at the last moment she may refuse to accompany me!"

"Perhaps I should come too," the Count said, "to prevent her from running away when she becomes really bored."

"There is an old adage that you have forgotten," the Marquis retorted, "that two's company and three is none!"

Listening to them sparring Lola thought that it was more amusing than anything she had heard for a long time.

They were teasing and arguing with each other, but whatever they said it always ended in laughter.

*

As the Count said goodbye to them the following morning before they drove to the station, Lola was quite sorry that he was not going with them.

She felt, in fact, that the Marquis was a little awe-inspiring and she still found herself thinking that he was older than he appeared.

'I must not do anything that he might disapprove of,' she thought. 'And I must be very careful that he is not ashamed of me as his supposed wife.'

Because he had planned every detail, she was not surprised when she came down to breakfast that he handed her a simple gold wedding ring.

"I hope it fits you," he remarked as Lola took it.

She put it on the third finger of her left hand and it fitted her exactly.

"I am also taking some of my mother's jewellery with me," the Marquis said. "I thought that it would look strange if, as my wife, you had none."

"I have some of my mother's," Lola replied, "but it will not be grand enough for anyone who is supposed to be the Marchioness of Halaton."

"That is exactly what I thought and I will keep it for safety in my case and tell you when you should wear it."

"Thank you," Lola answered meekly.

The wedding ring made her even more conscious that she was acting a part that both her father and mother would have disapproved of.

Of course she would be telling lies in pretending to be the Marquis's wife and, although she tried to think that she was acting in a very good cause, she still felt guilty.

It was all, however, very exciting.

Finally they set off in the Express to carry them to Dover.

It was on the way there that the Marquis told Lola that they would be travelling on what was known as the Calais-Nice-Rome Express.

"Should I have read about it?" Lola asked.

"No reason why you should," the Marquis replied. "It only began its career just a year ago in 1883 and it is the creation of a brilliant man called Georges Nagelmackers, of whom you may have heard."

Lola then remembered reading that he had built and owned the Continental Express Line and she gave a cry,

"Oh, I have heard of the Orient Express and that it is the most exciting and romantic train ever."

"It is certainly the most romantic of the European Expresses," the Marquis agreed, "and it is high time that something was done about them."

"I have heard that they were very uncomfortable."

"They were really appalling," the Marquis replied, "and most of them still are."

As Lola seemed interested, he explained,

"The compartments one travels and sleeps in have three large seats with padded backs. One pulls these down with a handle to make the bed. Then there are no sheets or blankets, but it's possible to hire a pillow from a porter, who wheels a trolley down the platform with clean white pillows hanging from a pole."

"Is that all they give you?" Lola asked.

"Anyone with sense travels with a warm rug. The ladies don't undress as it is not considered safe in case of accidents."

"But that does not happen the way we are going?" Lola said tentatively.

"Certainly not. There are sleeping cars that I have already booked and my valet has brought the food we shall require on the journey."

Lola had noticed, when they set off for the Station, that the carriage with the Marquis's valet seemed filled with a great deal of luggage.

She had been relieved by what the Marquis had told her that the only person on the journey who would know their identity was his valet and he was trusted implicitly.

"Higgins has been with me since I left Oxford," he said. "He was my batman for a short time in the Regiment and looks after me rather like a Nanny. In fact I have to tell him continually not to mollycoddle me."

Lola laughed.

"I cannot imagine anyone doing that to you."

The Marquis was not sure if that was a compliment or not, but he replied,

"Higgins will look after you too and I am sure that he will treat you exactly as if you were a child he has to care for and protect."

"I shall enjoy that when I have always had to take care of myself."

She was thinking that after her Nanny had left there had been no one to replace her and this was because they could not afford anyone extra in the cottage.

"You must tell me now that we have the time," the Marquis said, "about your childhood. I am very interested in how you learnt to embroider so beautifully."

Lola realised that he was now being inquisitive and thought that this could be dangerous.

And she replied after thinking quickly,

"We are going on a voyage of discovery. For me it is just as exciting as if I was Jason looking for the Golden Fleece. So what I want you to do is to tell me about Italy and, of course, more about your amazing engine."

"I will naturally be delighted to do so," the Marquis replied.

Lola knew, as if she could read his thoughts, that it was not what he really intended.

She told herself that she must be very careful and she must not say anything that might give him the idea that her uncle was just as important socially as he was.

She had worked it out for herself.

If the Marquis knew that she was the niece of the Earl of Kencombe, he would have second thoughts about employing her as an embroideress.

And he would most certainly not have asked her to act the part of his wife to deceive an Italian millionaire.

'He is clever,' she told herself, 'and he may try to learn things I don't want him to know. I must therefore be very cautious in what I say.'

The Marquis was provided with all the newspapers and a number of magazines and this saved her from having to talk on the journey to Dover.

When they arrived, they went aboard the Channel Steamer and were shown into a private cabin.

Lola guessed that it must be the largest and most expensive on board, but even so there was very little room after all their luggage had been brought in.

The Marquis said he wanted some sea air and so he walked round the deck the whole time they were crossing the English Channel.

Lola would have liked to join him, but she knew that it would be a mistake in case anyone should notice her.

Or, what was far more likely, wonder who it was accompanying the Marquis.

She was quite certain that he would be known at least by sight to somebody on board, either to a personal friend or to some member of the public as his picture was often in the newspapers.

She therefore sat quietly in the cabin gazing out of the window from time to time.

When they arrived at Calais, people rushed off the ship and made a mad dash to the buffet.

Lola wondered why they were in such a hurry and she learned later that they had only twenty-five minutes in which to eat a meal before the train left.

Without eating to worry them, the Marquis led the way to the platform where the Calais-Nice-Rome Express was waiting.

It was the largest and most impressive train that Lola had ever seen.

When she saw the sleeping cars, she realised just how lucky she was, as she might have been travelling in the discomfort that the Marquis had told her about.

She found her sleeping compartment delightful and very much what she had expected when she had read about the Orient Express.

Higgins arranged her luggage for her and found her a nightgown and negligée she would need that night.

Then he went off to look after the Marquis and now Lola could see from the window the passengers, who had been in the buffet, struggling with their luggage down the platform and searching with anxious faces at the various compartments for a comfortable seat.

She thought again how lucky she was to have a whole sleeping compartment to herself.

A little later on, when it was nearly dinnertime, she learned that a third compartment had been booked by the Marquis to act as a sitting room.

It had a bed, which was not made up, and their food was arranged on the seat between them while they were waited on by Higgins.

"This is really luxurious," Lola sighed.

"There is a dining car," the Marquis replied, "but it would be risky for us to eat there together."

Lola thought that this was indeed sensible, but she could not help give a little laugh.

"What do you find so amusing?" he asked.

"Because you do everything in such a grand style," she said, "and at the same time you think of every detail."

"I try. I also prefer my own food even though you might rather have a French meal."

"You know quite well nothing could be nicer than this," Lola said.

She had known ever since coming to Queen's Hoo that the food there was particularly good, again because the Marquis always demanded perfection.

She sipped the cooled champagne that Higgins had poured out for them and she only wished that she could tell her father and mother where she was at this moment.

When she retired to bed and found the berth very comfortable, she sent up a little prayer.

She prayed that her father and mother would not be angry with her for coming alone with the Marquis.

'It is all so thrilling and something I never thought I would be able to do, Mama!' she said in her heart. 'If no one ever knows the truth or talks about it, I cannot see that it will be very wrong. And besides, you and Papa will be looking after me.'

She was completely convinced that it was her father and mother who had somehow directed her to Mrs. Hill and then from Mrs. Hill to Mrs. Whicker.

Now she would be able to see what her father had always wished her to see, the places in Europe that they had read about together. He would also be delighted, she thought, that she could speak Italian so well.

She did not tell the Marquis that she could do so, as she thought it would make him all the more curious.

'I have so much to be grateful for and this is all so wonderful,' she reflected.

They reached Paris early in the morning and did not have to change trains.

Lola looked out at the Station and wished that there was some excuse for the Marquis to take her into Paris, as there was so much she wanted to see there, the Louvre, the *Champs Élysées*, the *Place de la Concorde* and, of course, the River Seine.

She had read about Paris and felt, because it had been so interesting, that she had already seen it.

How could she complain when she would be lucky enough to see the beauty of Florence with her own eyes and not just through books?

She thought that she was already familiar with the magnificent pictures in the Pitti and Uffizi Galleries and she had seen photographs of Florence and the River Arno flowing under bridges that carried shops above them.

'I so want to see everything,' she told herself, 'and perhaps like Papa I will write a book about it.'

It was certainly an idea, an idea which would make money so that she would be able to afford, with what the Marquis was giving her, to stay at her beloved home.

She would not have to embroider after she had left Queens Hoo until she had put everything down on paper that she would be seeing on this trip.

When the Marquis said goodnight to her after they had finished dinner, he said,

"I hope you sleep well, Miss – "

He was about to say 'Fenton,' when he stopped.

"We must start at once to call each other by our Christian names," he said.

Lola laughed.

"I had forgotten we should do that."

"The Italians would think it strange if we don't. As I expect you will now know, my Christian name is Kelvin and you told me when I applied for your passport that you are 'Lola'. And how did you get such an unusual name?"

"My father was writing a book at the time of my birth on Spain," she replied without thinking, "and Dolores is a Spanish name that he thought rather attractive."

"Then your father wrote books?"

She realised that she had made a mistake by saying this, especially as the Marquis went on,

"I wonder if I have any of them in my library."

"I think it is unlikely," Lola replied. "When we go back to Queens Hoo, I will look."

"Did your father write under his own name or under a *nom-de-plume*?" the Marquis enquired.

"Under his own name, but you will not have read any of his books because they were mostly on unusual and specialist subjects that few people are interested in."

The Marquis now noted in the back of his mind that Lola's father had not been a successful author and this was all part of the jigsaw he was piecing together about her.

Aloud he said,

"You make your father sound very erudite."

"That is just what he was, so you can understand that his books, which were really for Dons and professional Historians, did not have a large sale."

"Are you thinking of following his example, Lola?"

She felt strongly that he must have been reading her thoughts and replied,

"I will answer that question when we go home. I have read a great deal about Italy, which is not the same as seeing it for myself."

"No, of course not. It is a very beautiful country and, as you will know, extremely mountainous."

She knew that he was thinking now of his engine and, to divert his attention from herself, she said,

"It would be a great triumph, would it not, if you manage to produce an engine that can climb the Apennines without any difficulty?"

"That is what I hope to do. As I expect you know, England and America lead the world in the development of railways, but those that have opened in Italy have not been very successful."

"Why not?" Lola asked.

"I think the answer is simply lack of money and the special problems arising from the mountain range running down the centre of the country."

"Then if you can give them something that will be a success," Lola said, "they should be very grateful to you."

"I hope so," the Marquis smiled, "but you know as well as I do that people are not always ready to thank you for interfering when they are quite content to go on as they are doing."

"That is very true," Lola replied.

As they drew nearer to Italy, she grew more and more excited.

She found that the Marquis had brought with him a guide book, which she read from cover to cover. It told her so much about the country that she had not known before.

She also asked him a great number of questions and he thought as he tried to answer them that she was certainly intelligent.

And in fact very different from any woman he had travelled with in the past. They had been intent on holding his attention on them and were not interested in anything except when the conversation turned to love.

He was always vividly conscious of how exquisite Lola looked.

Not only in the evening, but even first thing in the morning when Higgins served their breakfast in the spare compartment that they had made into a sitting room.

He had always associated with much older beauties, and he could not help noticing how incredibly clear Lola's complexion was and how the sunshine streaming through the window glistened on her golden hair.

There was indeed no mascara on her eyelashes and they turned up like a child's and were a little darker at the ends than they were closer to the lids.

And there was no salve on her lips, which were the colour of the roses that grew in the garden at Queens Hoo.

106

Because she was so excited by everything she saw and everything he told her, her eyes were shining like stars.

'Camilo is so right,' the Marquis told himself, 'she is enchanting and I must be very careful that the Italians do not spoil her with their compliments.'

It struck him that they would undoubtedly attempt to flirt with her and he knew from the way he had seen her behave with the Count that she would have no idea what this meant and would feel embarrassed by compliments.

She was just so different from the women he had been with, who looked on compliments as their right and they were always fishing for more of them if they were not immediately forthcoming.

He did not pay Lola compliments, although often he found them trembling on his lips, but he thought as well that they might change her attitude towards him.

He was intelligent enough to know that she looked on him in the same way as she might on a Guardian or perhaps her father.

'It has,' he thought, 'never entered her mind that I am an attractive man and so she accepts what I say to her respectfully.'

Equally she was a bit like a child acknowledging his superiority because of age and it was rather a sobering thought.

The Marquis thought how many women had fallen into his arms, as the Count had said, like overripe peaches.

It seemed a little odd, if not extraordinary, that this young girl should regard him in such a different way.

'But it suits my purpose exactly,' he told himself.

Lola went to her own compartment at night without a backward glance.

The Marquis could not help thinking that no other women would have left him without inviting his kisses and inevitably a great deal more.

Lola's behaviour was, of course, exactly what he wanted, but even so it was somewhat strange.

'I must be getting old,' he mused, 'and sooner or later I shall have to consider having an heir and that entails finding a wife.'

He recalled the beauties he had been with when he was last in London, one or two in particular with whom he had spent a great deal of his time.

None of them were available for marriage.

Some of his many friends have *debutante* daughters and they have been paraded in front of him in the obvious hope that he would find one of them a suitable chatelaine of Queens Hoo.

'I would be bored to distraction in two months,' the Marquis thought when he looked at them.

He had to admit that surprisingly he had not been in the least bored by Lola since they had left London.

It was a very different journey alone with a woman from any he had ever spent before and he had expected to spend his time reading a book. He would then not have to make idiotic conversation with his companion.

Now, as they neared Italy, he had to admit that his book had remained unopened, except when he was alone.

He had found Lola to be interesting, amusing and extremely intelligent. They had discussed subjects like the difference between French characteristics and Italian.

He might, he felt, have been arguing a point with the Count or one of his friends in White's Club and, seeing how young she was, it seemed to him really extraordinary.

He had to admit that she was unique and Camilo had been right when he had said that she was ethereal.

As he rather fancied himself as a judge of beauty, he had to admit that every movement she made had a grace that he had not seen before in any other woman.

Her profile when she was gazing out of the window was flawless, as for that matter were her manners.

When they ate together, he knew that Mrs. Whicker had been right. Lola was a lady and it would have been wrong for her to eat with the staff.

Then who was she and why was she alone in the world?

The questions were back in his mind.

For the present, whether it was by her design or not, he had no answer to them.

CHAPTER SIX

Finally they reached Florence.

Lola could not help wondering as they drew nearer to meeting Signor Galvani if the Marquis felt nervous.

They had talked about his engine so often that by now she realised how much it meant to him and he would be desperately disappointed if he had to start all over again searching for someone to build it.

'I don't want him to be hurt or upset,' she mused.

She sent a special little prayer to God that Signor Galvani would not be furious when he discovered that the Marquis was married.

A smart carriage met them at Florence Station.

Signor Galvani was not there himself to welcome them, but his private secretary was undoubtedly surprised when he saw that the Marquis was not alone.

But there was no need to make any explanations to him and they drove off through the narrow crowded streets.

Lola was enchanted at her first sight of Florence, which was just as beautiful as she expected it to be.

They drove only a short way beside the Arno before they turned away from the river and the Marquis had told her that Signor Galvani's villa was high on the hills above the City.

It was a twisting uphill drive and the two horses that drew the carriage managed it without much difficulty.

Finally they reached a large and impressive-looking Villa from which there was a breathtaking view.

Lola was, however, more intent on noticing how the Marquis was received. Would it be, as she was afraid, a considerable shock to their host that she was with him?

A splendidly uniformed Major Domo showed them through an over-furnished hall and along a wide passage hung with fine pictures.

At the end of it he opened a door and, ignoring Lola, announced in Italian.

"The Most Noble the Marquis of Halaton."

Lola had a quick impression of a nicely furnished room with long windows opening onto a terrace and then she turned and saw Signor Antonio Galvani rising from the desk where he had been sitting.

As he walked towards the Marquis with his hand outstretched, she saw him look at her with surprise.

"I am delighted to see you," he said in Italian to the Marquis.

"And I am delighted and grateful to be here to meet you," the Marquis replied.

They shook hands and then the Marquis said,

"May I introduce you to my wife?"

Lola saw him draw in his breath before he queried,

"Your wife?"

The Marquis smiled.

"It may be a surprise to you, *signore*, as it will be to a great many others, but we have been married secretly since my wife is in mourning for a relation. Otherwise it would have meant having to wait for six months."

The Italian did not speak and the Marquis went on with a light laugh,

"Her Majesty, Queen Victoria, is most particular about long drawn out mourning."

"I had no idea that you would be married," Signor Galvani said doubtfully.

Lola thought that he spoke with some difficulty and to lighten the atmosphere she said,

"I do hope you will forgive me for coming with my husband, but I was so longing to see your beautiful country and, of course, to meet you."

She spoke in fluent Italian and was aware that the Marquis was looking at her in astonishment.

Signor Galvani managed to remark,

"So you speak my language?"

"It is as beautiful as the magnificent view from this window," Lola answered him.

They then sat down and, as if he could not wait, the Marquis began to talk eagerly about his engine.

Lola was watching Signor Galvani.

While being extremely polite, he was not showing the eagerness and interest that the Marquis had hoped for and Lola knew that it was because the Italian was upset at his plan being baulked.

They were offered glasses of an excellent wine and, as they drank Lola managed to pay effusive compliments to Signor Galvani and she knew that this was something the Marquis had not expected.

They were still talking when the door opened and a girl came in.

Lola guessed at once that this was Signor Galvani's daughter and she certainly was extremely pretty and most presentable.

She thought that her black hair and large dark eyes would have attracted any man, unless he was concerned, like the Marquis, only with how blue-blooded and English his wife must be.

Battista, as she was called, was not in the least shy at meeting strangers and she also did not seem in the least perturbed to learn that the Marquis was married.

After her arrival Signor Galvani became extremely aloof and then he began to answer the Marquis's questions about his engine in monosyllables.

'He is going to refuse to build it,' Lola thought to herself and she wondered frantically what she could do.

She was still thinking when Signor Galvani said,

"I am sure, my Lady, you would like to rest before dinner at nine. Battista will show you to your room which, of course, as you are married, will have to be altered as I had expected your husband to sleep alone."

There was definitely a hard note in his voice when he said the last words and Lola could only reply,

"Thank you, *signore*, I would like to rest and I do apologise if I have upset your household arrangements."

"There is no reason at all for your Ladyship to apologise," Signor Galvani replied politely.

As he was speaking, the Marquis walked over to the open window and stood looking out.

"What a fantastic view you have," he exclaimed.

Battista joined him and pointed out the Cathedral and various other towers and spires in the distance.

As she was doing so, Lola had an idea.

Drawing a little nearer to Signor Galvani, she said,

"How pretty your daughter is! You must let her come and stay with us in England. I am quite sure that she would be a sensation in London Society."

Signor Galvani looked at her in some surprise.

Then he said,

"Are you seriously suggesting that Battista should stay with you?"

"We would be delighted to have her," Lola replied, "but I am afraid, because I am in mourning as my husband has told you, she will have to wait until the autumn. Then she can not only attend balls in London but I will persuade my husband to give one for her at Queens Hoo."

The whole attitude of the Italian altered and now it appeared as if his enthusiasm and interest in the Marquis returned like a floodtide.

As he joined him at the open window, he said,

"Even at this height you can well understand that we will need an electric engine like yours."

The Marquis had heard all that Lola had said and replied,

"That is exactly what I wanted you to say, *signore*."

"We will talk about it after dinner," Signor Galvani promised.

He himself escorted them upstairs with Battista and showed them into a large beautifully furnished room which had a balcony and the same magnificent view.

There was a small dressing room leading off it for the Marquis and a boudoir where Signor Galvani pointed out they could write their letters without being disturbed.

"No matter how many letters I write," Lola said, "I could never describe adequately the beauty of Italy as I can see it from here."

"I will show you other places as beautiful," Signor Galvani replied, "and with your husband's interest in my country there are many towns to visit besides Florence."

'It is extraordinary,' Lola thought, 'the difference in him now he has made up his mind to accept the situation.'

She continued to pay him even more compliments and told Battista how beautiful she was before they finally left them alone.

When he was sure that they were out of hearing, the Marquis lowered his voice to say,

"Thank you, Lola, that was so very clever of you."

"I was sure," she whispered, "that he was going to refuse to build your engine when he knew that there was no chance of you marrying his daughter."

"I was well aware of that," the Marquis replied, "I was wondering frantically how I could save the day when you did it for me!"

He smiled before he went on,

"Being just as lovely as you are, there is really no reason for you to have such a clever little brain as well!"

"It comes in useful at times," Lola replied lightly.

She went to the window to gaze again at the view.

"Could anything be lovelier?" she asked.

The Marquis wondered whether he should say, as he would have to any other woman, that she was indeed even lovelier.

Then he bit back the words. He did not want to make her feel self-conscious, but he was well aware how intelligent she had been.

He had known, even more acutely than Lola had, that, when he arrived with a wife, Signor Galvani had not only been surprised but very angry.

It was not what he said. It was the anger in his eyes and the hostile vibrations that emanated from him.

The Marquis had been wondering frantically how he could influence him, knowing that he was so rich that money was not of any consequence to him.

Then Lola, when he least expected it, had brought the Italian round as if by the touch of a magic wand.

'It may be difficult,' he thought, 'when the time comes for me to invite Battista to England. I will have to think of a reason why my wife is no longer with me.'

There was, however, no point in trying to jump that fence until he came to it.

By that time, he hoped, the engine would have been built and in service and there would be nothing that Signor Galvani could then do to circumvent it.

"I just cannot tell you how grateful I am to you," he enthused again to Lola.

"Be very careful," she said lowering her voice. "I can see he is a very difficult man and, if he has even the slightest suspicion that we are deceiving him, he may hurt you in a great many ways."

"I am aware of that," the Marquis answered.

Lola went to her bedroom where two maid-servants were unpacking her clothes.

Because she was tired after the long journey, she undressed and climbed into bed and told them to call her in plenty of time so that she would not be late for dinner.

She guessed that the Marquis would be downstairs talking to Signor Galvani about his engine.

However, there was no need to worry about him and now he would able to try to put his plan into operation as quickly as possible.

She slept for a little while and when she was called she put on one of her prettiest dresses.

She had left it to the Marquis, as they had arranged, to explain that, although in mourning, she had decided as they were not on their honeymoon to wear coloured clothes and not black.

And she could not help hoping that Signor Galvani would not think her trousseau rather shabby. Her mother's gown was pretty but not particularly expensive.

As if the Marquis had thought the same thing, he knocked on the communicating door.

When Lola said, 'come in', he entered with a jewel-case in his hands and the maid who had been waiting on her tactfully withdrew.

When she had closed the door, the Marquis said,

"I have brought my mother's jewellery. Galvani will expect you to glitter as my wife and so we must not disappoint him."

"I will be very careful with it," Lola promised.

The Marquis opened the jewel-case and brought out a necklace of large diamonds and earrings to match.

"They are lovely!" Lola exclaimed. "And I do hope up here in the hills they are safe from thieves. I believe there are a great number in Florence itself."

"I had thought of that. Whatever jewels you are not wearing, I will lock away where it is unlikely that thieves will look for them."

There was a bracelet for Lola's wrist and a ring set with a very large diamond.

"Now I can really admire myself," she said, looking in the mirror. "Thank you so much for trusting me with such precious jewels."

"They certainly become you," he said and, turning, he then went back through the communicating door.

He was thinking that she looked so beautiful that he had an almost irresistible urge to kiss her.

'She would not understand,' he reflected, 'and it would upset the sensible and practical relationship we now have with each other.'

Lola had not been prepared for a party, but the Italian wanted to show off the importance of his guest.

There were therefore a number of pretty women with distinguished husbands, in fact the *crème de la crème* of Florence, and they sat down twenty for dinner.

The Marquis, of course, could not talk about his train as it was a secret known only to Signor Galvani.

Lola thought that it was a lovely party. She had been to so few and she was engulfed by all the extravagant compliments paid to her by the two Italians who sat either side of her.

Everyone was astonished that she spoke such good Italian and, when the party was over, Signor Galvani said,

"I can only thank you, my Lady, for making my dinner party a special occasion that will be talked about and remembered long after you have left Florence."

He kissed her hand.

As Lola went up the stairs, she thought that she had never enjoyed herself more.

'It's a case,' she mused, 'of rags to riches and I can only hope that it will last a long time!'

She slept peacefully in a very comfortable bed.

*

The next day the Marquis was going into endless details over the building of his engine with Signor Galvani, while Lola and Battista went out together and visited the Pitti and Uffizi Galleries.

They also had time to go into the Cathedral so that Lola could say a prayer and light a candle and she added to her gratitude a plea that they would not be found out.

Her uncle must never know what a wonderful time she was having in pretending to be the wife of the Marquis!

When they returned to the Villa, Lola knew from the expression on the Marquis's face that everything had gone well.

There was no opportunity of speaking to him alone, as there were people coming during the afternoon whom Signor Galvani particularly wanted them to meet.

It was time to dress for dinner before Lola had a chance of having a word with the man who was supposed to be her husband.

There was to be another dinner party that night and, when she had put on another of her mother's dresses, she waited for him to come through the communicating door.

Tonight, having asked what she would be wearing, he brought her a necklace of sapphires with the earrings and bracelets to match.

They were, he thought, only a little darker than the colour of her eyes and they became her even more than the diamonds.

Lola stood up to look at herself in the mirror.

"Thank you," she sighed, "for these lovely jewels, do I look all right?"

She turned and the Marquis drew in his breath.

As he was about to speak, there was the sound of wheels outside and they knew that carriages were driving up to the front of the house.

"We must hurry downstairs," he urged.

The party was as amusing as the night before and, because it was Saturday, the guests left early.

Lola guessed that, as they were all Catholics, they would all be going to Mass early on Sunday morning.

When she reached her room, she put the sapphires back into their velvet-lined boxes and hid them away in the back of a drawer in her dressing table.

She climbed into bed and was about to blow out the candle beside her, when the communicating door opened.

The Marquis came in.

He was wearing a long dark robe and she realised that he was undressed and ready for bed.

"What is the matter?" she asked. "Is there anything wrong?"

He reached the side of her bed before he answered,

"There is nothing wrong, I came to say goodnight to you and also to make a suggestion."

"A suggestion?" she queried in surprise.

The Marquis sat down on the side of her bed, which she thought was rather strange.

He looked serious and again she asked,

"Has anything upset you? Has the Signore decided after all not to make your engine?"

"No, it is nothing like that."

The Marquis bent forward to take her hand in his.

"I was thinking today," he said, "even when I was working on my engine, how beautiful you are."

"You can hardly expect me to believe that," Lola replied. "When you are thinking of your engine, there is no room in your mind for anything else."

"Actually there is you, Lola, and I have indeed been thinking about you a great deal. I have, as I have already said, a suggestion that I hope you will agree to."

"What is it?" she asked.

She wondered why he was still holding her hand and at the same time it was something she enjoyed.

She could not explain it, but, when he touched her, she felt a little tremor go through her.

Now she was very conscious of the strength of his fingers and that he was a very good-looking man.

"I don't have to tell you," the Marquis was saying in a deep voice, "that you are acting the part of my wife with a brilliance that is difficult to express in words."

Lola gave a little sigh of relief.

"I have been so afraid of doing the wrong thing,"

"You have been perfect and it is perfection I always look for."

"That is what I want to hear," Lola smiled, "and I hope that you will remember it when I go back to being just your embroideress."

"That is just what I want to talk to you about," the Marquis said. "Because I am so happy with you, I want to be happier still."

Lola did not understand and he went on,

"You must be well aware that I cannot offer you marriage, because my family would never accept you and I have to marry someone who is my equal socially."

It flashed through Lola's mind that she had never thought of marrying him, but now he was being somewhat insulting.

"So what I want to suggest," the Marquis went on, "because I find you so adorable or perhaps the right word is 'irresistible', is that we could be very happy together."

"I – really don't know – what you are saying," she stammered.

"I promise you," the Marquis said, "that you shall have everything in the world you want and you will never have to work again. I will give you a house in London and I will be with you as much as possible. I know, feeling as I do now, that it will be difficult for us ever to be apart."

"I don't know what you are saying," she murmured. "I don't – understand."

"Then let me make it a little clearer. I want you as a man wants a woman. In fact I love you and so it will be impossible for me to let you go."

Lola then took her hand from his and, pulling up the sheet over her breasts, she held it against her as if for protection.

"Are – you," she said in a very small voice, "asking me to be – your mistress?"

"That is such a harsh word for something that can be very beautiful and make us both very happy. As I have already said, I will give you everything in the world it is possible for me to give."

He moved a bit closer to Lola as he spoke, but she pressed herself back against the pillows.

"No! No! Of course not. How could you think of anything so wrong, so wicked? Both my father and mother would be shocked at what you have just said."

"Your father and mother," the Marquis said, "have left you alone in the world with no money. I think that they would be pleased for someone like me to look after you and see that never again would you have to go to an Agency to find work."

It flashed through Lola's mind that she could tell him why she had gone to the Agency and why she was avoiding her uncle who, however unpleasant he might be, was the equal of the Marquis socially.

Then she knew that what the Marquis was offering was not love.

Not the love that her mother had had for her father. She had given up everything for him and she had lived in penury compared with what she had enjoyed at her home.

That Neville Fenton had been the paid servant of her grandfather was what the family could not forgive. It had not mattered to her mother, for she had loved him as he had loved her and they had been, as Lola knew, supremely happy without the blessing of the family.

The Marquis was waiting for her answer and she was aware that he was drawing nearer to her.

It was only a matter of seconds before he would put out his arms and, she feared, kiss her.

"Go away!" she cried. "Go away at once! You have no right to come into my bedroom and suggest something that would shock my mother and make my father turn you out of the house."

"Now listen, Lola – " the Marquis began again.

"I am not going to listen to you," Lola interrupted, "and I want to go back – to England."

"You know you cannot do that. You cannot let me down when everything is going so well."

"Then you are not to talk – to me about doing – things that I know are wrong and very very degrading."

"Please don't feel like that," the Marquis protested, "and I have already told you that I love you."

There was a little twist to his lips as he added,

"I fought against it because of the difference in our positions, but now I can only say that I love you as I have never loved any woman before and I want to protect you and make you happy."

"But what you are suggesting is not the right way to make me happy – or to protect me from what people would say and think if they knew that I was your – mistress."

Because the last word shocked her, she said it in a low frightened voice.

"I don't want you to feel like that, Lola. I love you and, as I have already said, I know that we could be happy together if only you will let me look after you and save you from ever being penniless again."

"If I was ashamed of what I was doing and – knew that my mother and father were ashamed of me too, do you think – I could be happy?" Lola asked him.

She made a sound which was a cry of despair.

"Go away, go away and forget that you ever came in here and suggested anything so horrible and – wicked. I was so very happy and now you have ruined – *everything*."

The Marquis rose from the bed.

"I have never forced myself on any woman who is unwilling. But if you will allow me to kiss you, Lola, then I believe you will understand better what I am suggesting than you do at this moment."

"Go away!" Lola said. "You are frightening me. I am all alone in a strange country with no one to turn to and no money – so I cannot run away."

He made a rather helpless gesture with his hands.

"I have no wish to upset you, so I will go away as you have asked me to. But when you are alone, Lola, think over what I have suggested and I hope that you will begin to understand that it is a much more practical way of living than the way you are at the moment."

"What I am doing at the moment," Lola flashed, "is acting a lie and that is why God is punishing me by letting you ask me to do even – worse things!"

Her voice broke and now the tears were running down her cheeks.

The Marquis took a step forward as if he would take her in his arms and then he knew that it would upset her even more than she was already.

"I will leave you," he said. "Go to sleep and forget all this has happened. We will start again in the morning where we left off and you will tell me that you have never been so happy."

"You have spoilt – it all," Lola sobbed, "you have spoilt the fun we were having together and even seeing the beauty of Italy – will not be the same."

'She is speaking like an unhappy child,' he thought and he could not imagine what he could do about it.

"Forgive me, Lola," he said. "In the morning we will start again where we left off."

He walked to the communicating door and when he reached it he looked back and saw Lola turn round and hide her face in the pillows.

He knew that she was crying tempestuously.

He wanted to go back and take her in his arms and hold her close against him and yet he was aware that this would only make things worse.

With a sigh he went into the dressing room shutting the door behind him.

Lola cried for a long time.

Then, as her tears ceased, she wiped her eyes and tried to think clearly.

What the Marquis had just proposed had shocked her as she had never been shocked before in her quiet life.

Then she thought the problem over practically, as her father had told her always to do.

She understood from the Marquis's point of view that it was the only thing that he could offer her.

She knew only too well the way that her family had behaved towards her mother.

No one would have doubted for a moment, except, Lola thought bitterly, the Combes, that Neville Fenton was a gentleman born and bred and there was no real reason why he should not have married her mother.

His father was a country Squire and his ancestors went back for many generations.

Neville had been educated at one of the very best schools and had gone on to one of the best Universities, yet that he was employed as a Tutor put him at once into a very different category as far as the Earl of Kencombe was concerned.

He was in his eyes a paid servant and that he should approach his daughter was, he considered, an insult.

In a fury he had driven Neville Fenton away from Kencombe Park, saying that he never wished to see him again and added that he would not give him a reference as being a proper person to teach a child.

When Lady Cecilia had gone off with him, it had stunned not only her father but the whole family.

To them she had degraded herself unbelievably and they all agreed that the Earl must do the only possible thing in disowning her. He had even refused to have her name mentioned in his presence.

That is just, Lola now thought, how the Marquis's family would feel if he said that he was intending to marry an embroideress in his employment

Then, as she thought more about him, she suddenly realised that she wanted to marry the Marquis.

She had not realised that the agony she had felt about him was love.

Now she knew that, if he had kissed her, it might have been very difficult for her to send him away and to tell him that what he had suggested was wrong and wicked.

'I love him,' she said to herself with a little sob, 'at the same time he does not really love me.'

If he had loved her in the same way that her mother had loved her father, he would have offered her marriage, but she could understand his reason for not doing so.

She knew that if she told him who she was, it might change everything.

Yet could she ever be happy with a man who did not really love her.

There were no obstacles to real love, there was only the need for the person to be loved.

'I will go away,' she thought, 'and then I will never need to see him again.'

To think about it was almost like a dagger being driven into her heart and she wanted to cry out at the pain of it.

It was no use pretending – she loved him with her heart and also with her soul.

She knew now that she had been aware of it when they were in the train and talking together.

She had thought that nothing could ever make her happier or more thrilled.

But, because she had never known love, she did not realise exactly what she was feeling.

She had wanted the time they talked together after dinner to last for the whole night and more.

When she went to bed in her own compartment, she was counting the hours until she could see him again.

'Why did I not realise that it was love?' she asked herself.

Then it was as if the devil was tempting her.

She had only to cross over the room to where he was sleeping and tell him that she had changed her mind.

'I love you, I do love you,' she would say, 'and because I know that I will never love anyone in the same way, I will do as you suggest.'

She could imagine his arms going round her and his lips finding hers.

She had never been kissed and if the Marquis did kiss her it would be like being taken up into Heaven.

Then her mother was standing beside her and Lola knew that she would not approve of anything that was so wrong and so wicked.

"I will try not to, Mama," she cried out aloud, "but help me. Help me to go on being with him, but not to give in."

She felt that her mother would understand as she added,

"I know now that I love him as you loved Papa. But only half of him loves me and he thinks that I am not good enough to be the Marchioness of Halaton except in pretence."

She wondered how tomorrow she would ever be able to go on acting as well as she had done today.

The tears came back into her eyes.

*

Lola slept a little before dawn and, when she woke, the question was back in her mind as to what she should do.

How would she be able to resist the Marquis if he went on pressing her to let him look after her as he wanted.

She had an idea that she must pray even harder than she had done during the night.

It was still early in the morning and she dressed herself quickly without ringing for the maid.

Lola remembered that, when they were driving up the hill to the Villa Galvani, she had seen a little Church by the roadside.

There had been a holy statue outside it, which had attracted her attention and she had pointed it out to the Marquis.

"You will see statues like that one all over Italy," he told her, "and, of course, you must see the Cathedral in Florence before we leave."

There was no chance at the moment of going to the Cathedral, but Lola felt that she must pray in a consecrated place.

If she did, God would give her the strength to fight against her own heart and He would help her to remain pure and untouched as her mother would want her to be.

It was warm so she just wore a light jacket over her gown.

She put on a small hat, opened the door and went down the stairs.

A footman in shirt sleeves was polishing the floor and he looked at Lola in surprise as she said,

"I am just going to the little Church I saw as I came up the hill."

The man smiled,

"Tis Father Marco who preaches there, *signora*, he a very good and holy man."

It passed through her mind that she might consult the Priest.

Then she remembered that she was playing a part and it would be dangerous to admit, even to a Priest, that she was pretending to be the wife of the Marquis.

"I shall not be long," she said.

The footman pulled back the bolt and opened the door and, as he did so, rather clumsily, he cut his finger.

He put it in his mouth as it was obviously bleeding and Lola said to him,

"You must be very careful. You have cut yourself and you must not get dirt in it."

"It'll be all right, *signora*," he replied.

Lola looked in her handbag and drew out a clean linen handkerchief.

"Let me see it," she asked him.

He then held out his finger and she saw that he had broken the skin and blood was oozing from it. She mopped it up carefully and then, knowing it was clean, she tied her handkerchief round it.

"You must keep it on until it stops bleeding and be very careful not to let any dirt into the wound."

The footman smiled at her.

"That is very kind of you, *signora*," he said.

She then hurried through the door down the drive and through the elegant gates at the entrance.

There was a small stretch of winding road before she saw the Church ahead of her.

She had been aware, as soon as she left the drive, that there were two men behind her on the road.

Now, although she was walking quickly, they must have accelerated and came up on either side of her.

She looked at one to see that he was a rather coarse rough-looking man and did not look at all like an Italian.

She glanced at the other man and realised that he was of the same type.

She wondered who they were and thought it strange that they were walking beside her.

Then just ahead, outside the small Church, she saw a closed carriage and supposed that she would not be the only person worshipping at this early hour of the morning.

Then, just as she reached the carriage, the two men closed in upon her and took hold of her arms.

"What are you – doing? Don't touch me!" she cried in Italian.

There was no answer and she found herself being propelled forcibly towards the carriage.

A man who was standing beside it opened the door and, as they pushed Lola into it, she screamed.

Then, as one of the other men joined her inside the carriage, the door was shut and it moved off.

"What is – happening? What are you doing?" Lola cried.

She had been half thrown on the back seat and now she was trying to raise herself.

The man sitting opposite did not answer and then she exclaimed again,

"What are you doing? Who are you and where are – you taking me?"

The carriage quickened its pace and then it flashed through Lola's mind that she had been kidnapped.

CHAPTER SEVEN

"Where are you – taking me?" she called out again, trying to keep her voice steady.

The man sitting opposite to her did not answer and after a moment she enquired in a more frightened tone,

"Please tell me – why you are doing this to me?"

Maybe because she sounded rather pathetic the man replied,

"Your husband. Very rich, we want money!"

Lola looked at him and was certain that he was not an Italian, as there was something about him that seemed rather coarse.

Suddenly she said, almost thinking aloud,

"Are you Macedonian?"

To her surprise the man gave her what might have been called a smile.

"That right. I Macedonian partisan."

Lola felt a fear shake her and she now understood what was happening.

The Macedonians had been fighting for centuries and they had in fact been very badly treated.

Only six years ago a new and independent State of Bulgaria incorporating most of Macedonia had been set up by the Russians through a Treaty with Turkey.

She recalled her father being very annoyed about it and he had told her that Great Britain had denounced the Treaty as unfair to the Greeks of Macedonia.

Neville Fenton had always been on the side of the Greeks wherever they lived in the Balkan Peninsula and he had been delighted when some of the territory grabbed by the Russians had been recovered.

Lola had realised from all that he had said that the Macedonians were determined to fight back in every way they could.

She knew now why she had been kidnapped, but it was a terrifying thought in case they ill-treated her.

The carriage was going downhill and was moving slowly and she wondered if she could throw herself out.

She knew that the man inside with her and the man beside the driver could easily prevent her from escaping.

It was what seemed to Lola a long time before the carriage came to a standstill and then the man beside her jumped out and pulled her after him.

She saw that they were in front of an obviously uninhabited villa.

The pillars outside it were broken, the glass in the windows was smashed and it was much too dilapidated for human habitation.

The man took her arm and dragged her through the front door and then they crossed a hall where the staircase was broken and so was a marble fireplace.

They went down a passage with bare boards that were loose and creaked beneath their feet.

Finally at the end of it the other man went forward to open a door and, when they passed through, Lola's heart sank.

It was a room she thought at first without windows and then she saw that either the shutters were closed or the windows had been boarded up.

There was an iron bedstead at one end of the room, a chair and table, but otherwise the room was empty.

The man still holding her arm dragged her towards the table and she saw writing-paper on it, an ink-pot and a quill pen.

"Write!" he demanded in bad Italian. "You write, ask husband pay for you."

Lola knew from the way they were looking at her that there was no point in arguing and she had heard in the past how people had been abducted and held to ransom for huge sums of money.

She thought how angry the Marquis would be when he received her letter.

She sat down meekly on the chair and picked up the quill pen and, as she started to write, her two captors were whispering and she reckoned that they were discussing the price they would ask for her.

When the man told her what it was harshly in his abrupt voice, she gave a little cry.

"You cannot ask as much as that!" she exclaimed.

What they were demanding was in English money nearly twenty thousand pounds.

And how could the Marquis possibly pay so much for someone who did not really belong to him?

"It is too – much," she faltered.

"You write!" the man retorted gruffly.

Meekly she did as she was told and at the end of the letter she added in all sincerity,

"*I am sorry, I am so very sorry.*"

She signed her name.

The elder of the two men scrutinised her letter very slowly as if he suspected that she was trying to trick them in some way.

Lola had no idea where she was, except that it was down in the valley and she could not think of any way that she could tell the Marquis where she had been taken.

The man reading her letter seemed satisfied and he then folded the writing paper and put it down on the table.

"Write name, husband," he ordered abruptly.

Lola did as she was told and then they walked out of the room.

They shut the door and Lola heard the key turn in the lock.

Then she put her hands to her face in despair. She wanted to cry and scream at what had happened, but she knew that it would be useless.

From what she had read about people who had been kidnapped, they were often beaten into submission.

'What can I do? What can I do?' she asked herself and she knew that the answer was nothing.

She sat down on the bed, which had a coarse straw mattress covered by two thin blankets that were, much to her relief, fairly clean. And there was a bolster instead of pillows for her head.

At the moment she could only sit there praying for the Marquis to save her and she also prayed that he would not be too angry at being asked for such an enormous sum of money.

Perhaps he would send for the Police and perhaps they would have some idea of where the Macedonians had taken her.

Then she remembered that the Marquis would not on any account want any publicity and the fact that the Marchioness of Halaton had been kidnapped would be an international Press story.

It would certainly go into the English newspapers and she could easily imagine the consternation amongst his relatives.

Signor Galvani would then learn how he had been deceived.

'The Marquis will have to pay that enormous sum for me,' Lola thought despairingly.

He said that he loved her and that he would give her everything she wanted.

But that was only if she did what he required.

Paying twenty thousand pounds for a woman who had rejected him would be a very different matter.

All these endless questions, difficulties and dangers kept turning over and over in her mind.

She could only sit miserably in her prison.

The only light came from a small skylight over one of the windows that jutted out a little from the rest in the room.

At what Lola thought must be around midday, one of the Macedonians came in carrying a tray and he put it down on the table.

She saw that there was something to eat on it and a glass containing water.

"We very good to you," he said, "but no money, no food."

"If you starve me," Lola retorted, "I shall die and then – you will get nothing."

The man gave a sharp laugh.

"Husband very rich, you pretty, he pay."

He went from the room, turning the key in the lock as he had before.

Lola thought that receiving any compliment in the circumstances was hardly something she could appreciate, especially from a man who was asking for such a huge sum from her supposed husband.

She felt that there must be something she could do, but had no idea what it could be.

She prayed for her father to help her and he would no doubt understand clearly that the Macedonians wanted money above everything.

Perhaps this was the only way they could obtain it.

*

The hours dragged by and, if she was waiting, she supposed that the Macedonians were waiting too.

She wondered how they would arrange to collect the money if the Marquis was prepared to give it to them.

She recalled reading that kidnappers usually wanted their ill-gotten gains put somewhere remote like the foot of a mountain or inside a Church and anyway it would not be a place where they would be noticed and arrested.

She decided to lie down on the bed as it was hot and the room had no ventilation.

She took off her jacket and was determined when night came not to undress any further.

Maybe the Marquis would find a wonderful way of rescuing her and yet she could not imagine how.

Dusk came and the little light that she had in the room began to fade.

The door opened suddenly and she sat up.

It was only her jailer with another tray.

As he crossed the room, Lola quizzed him eagerly,

"Have you heard from my husband?"

He shook his head.

"Perhaps not want you."

It was almost a snarl and, because he looked at her angrily, Lola shrank away from him.

He put the food, which was much the same as what he had brought her before, down on the table.

"Money not come tomorrow," he snarled, "we send your finger."

Lola gave a cry.

"You cannot be so cruel! How could you possibly do anything – so horrid?"

He did not answer, but strutted across the room and shut the door behind him.

For the first time Lola was afraid that the Marquis would not save her and perhaps he was so angry at the way she had behaved last night that he would just abandon her.

If she was not found, she would be presumed dead.

She tortured herself with the idea and finally she put her hands up to her eyes to wipe away the tears.

'I love him, I love him,' she cried to herself. 'Why was I so silly as not to do as he wanted?'

Because she was hungry she ate a little of the stale food that the Macedonian had brought her

To her surprise the man came back an hour later and took away the tray. He also brought a lighted candle in a tumbler, which he put down on the table.

"No answer!" he said curtly, as if Lola had asked the question.

"I expect," she said, "my husband – will have some difficulty in finding so much money and will have to wait until the banks – open in the morning."

The Macedonian did not reply, but she knew from the expression on his face that he understood.

He left the room and she fancied that he had gone to tell his friends what she had said.

It was very quiet and now there was nothing to do except to lie down.

Lola was praying again to the Marquis, praying that he would come and save her.

'I love you – I love you,' she whispered. '*Save me*!'

She must have fallen into a fitful asleep because she was dreaming of the Marquis when there was a faint sound that wakened her from her dream.

She opened her eyes in alarm.

Much of the candle had burned away and it was now below the level of the glass it stood in.

Then came the sound that she had heard before and she wondered what it could be.

She could not imagine that the man was returning to bring her anything or to see if she was comfortable and the sound she had heard was definitely not the key turning in the lock.

There was an even louder sound and she sat up on the bed.

Now it was frightening and she looked round at the windows wondering if someone was trying to open them.

Then to her astonishment she saw the boards in the centre of the floor moving.

A moment later they tipped up like a trapdoor.

Then she could see a hand moving them forward on the floor.

She held her breath, unable to move.

Up through the opening in the floor came a man's head.

It was the Marquis!

Lola would have given a cry of sheer joy and relief if he had not put a finger to his lips.

Slowly and carefully, so as not to make a sound, he drew himself up into the room.

He stepped onto the floor and came towards her.

Only then she moved from the bed and ran towards him.

She threw herself against him and his arms went round her.

Then, as if he was afraid that she would speak, his lips were on hers.

It was exactly what she had been dreaming about and longing for before she went to sleep.

And now it had actually happened!

The Marquis was kissing her and nothing else in the world could ever matter.

He was there and she was in his arms.

He kissed her until she felt as if they were being encompassed by the light of the sun.

Then, as he raised his head, his fingers were on her lips telling her again to be silent.

He drew her towards the opening in the floor.

Still without uttering a single word he then lowered himself down into it and held out his arms.

She bent towards him and he lifted her down.

She found that they were standing in a dark passage and there was a lantern on the ground beside them.

He pulled the trap door back into place and took a little time in closing it very carefully.

She thought it was so that no one would realise how she had escaped.

The Marquis picked up a lantern and walked ahead beckoning Lola to follow him.

She kept as close to him as she could in the narrow passage they were going down, but it was impossible for them to walk side by side.

The passage seemed to be taking them deeper down with every step they took and Lola felt that they must be going into the bowels of the earth.

Finally the passage came to an end.

They stepped out of it and she could see where they were.

There were bushes hiding the entrance, but straight ahead she could see in the moonlight the shining silver of water and knew that they must be on the banks of the Arno.

The Marquis carried his lantern in one hand and held out the other to Lola.

She slipped her hand into his and felt the strength of his fingers on her skin.

He had saved her and his kiss was still burning on her lips.

The Marquis walked forward, moving quickly as if, she thought, he was afraid that they might be seen.

Then, just in front of them, there was what looked like a large boat.

When they drew nearer, she saw that it was a small yacht and there were several seamen waiting to help them aboard.

As none of them spoke and neither did the Marquis, Lola knew that she must still keep silent too.

Almost as soon as they had stepped on board, the yacht began to move.

The Marquis took her below and into a cabin.

She just had time to see at a glance that it was well furnished before the Marquis, who had left the lantern he was holding at the top of the companionway, put his arms round her.

"My darling, my sweet," he said, "They have not hurt you?"

Lola found her voice.

"*You saved me!*" she cried. "I prayed and prayed that you would come – but felt you could not hear me."

"Of course I heard you."

Then he was kissing her. Kissing her possessively, demandingly and now holding her closer and closer to him.

It made Lola feel as if she had suddenly entered Paradise.

Nothing in the world could be as marvellous as the Marquis's kisses.

As the yacht was gathering speed, the Marquis sat down on the bed and pulled Lola down beside him.

"I love you, Lola," he breathed. "I will never let anything like this happen to you again."

"But you saved me," Lola said again. "How could you be so clever? How did you know where I was?"

"We were very very lucky," the Marquis explained. "It was the footman you were kind to and bandaged his finger, who told Galvani and me where you were."

"You received my letter? I was horrified that they should ask for so much money."

The Marquis smiled.

"I guessed you realised that they were Macedonians and they had intended to kidnap me."

"*You!* How could they think of such a thing?"

"Galvani talked too loudly about his distinguished guest," the Marquis replied, "and the Macedonians thought that it was an opportunity to hold to ransom a man they thought must be a millionaire."

"I don't understand how the footman knew where I was," Lola said.

"He too is a Macedonian and a partisan. He got a job in Galvani's household because they knew that he was very rich. But they dared not kidnap him for the simple reason that he is so well known in Italy. So they thought a foreigner would not cause such a commotion."

"So they were really waiting for you when I went – to the Church."

"Exactly. They had it all planned that being English I would be found looking at the garden. They would be waiting for me there to take me away at pistol point."

"Instead – they grabbed me," Lola murmured.

"I don't think that I have ever been so distraught as when you did not come back when I was told that you had gone to the Church. I learnt from the Priest that he had not seen you."

"What did you think had happened?" she enquired.

"I tried not to think the worst," the Marquis replied. "Then, when your letter came, which was discovered lying in the porch at ten o'clock in the morning, I was frantic."

He paused for a moment as if he was remembering how horrifying it had been.

"I felt I wanted to send for the Police, but I knew that might easily cause a scandal and inevitably it would be known sooner or later that I did not have a wife."

"I thought of that," Lola said.

"I was wondering if there was any alternative," the Marquis continued, "when the Macedonian footman asked to see me alone."

"And he told you what had happened?"

"He told me frankly that he was a partisan, but he did not like what he was doing and wanted to be married.

143

Lola smiled.

"In other words he wanted money."

"Of course he did and it was much less than what his friends were asking."

"I am so glad, so very glad. I could not bear to think of you having to give such an enormous sum for me."

"I would have given that and a million times more."

She looked up at him, their eyes met and he said very quietly,

"I love you, my darling, but you have been through a ghastly experience and I want you to go to sleep."

"I have not asked where we are going," Lola asked.

The Marquis smiled.

"It's a secret and I will tell you about it tomorrow."

He then kissed her again very gently as if she was infinitely precious.

Then, before she realised what was happening, he left the cabin and closed the door behind him.

She wanted to run after him and make him tell her more, but she realised that he had made his plans and she must not upset them.

She undressed and found to her surprise that there was one of her own nightgowns lying on the berth.

She put it on thinking that as they had left the Villa the Marquis must have brought their luggage with them.

'Maybe we are going back to England,' she thought and felt her spirits soar.

If that was what he was planning, they would soon be back at Queens Hoo and once again she would be just an embroideress for his cherished curtains.

Then, because she could still feel the Marquis's lips on hers, she thought only of his kisses until she fell asleep.

She was woken by someone knocking on the door.

He said in Italian that breakfast would be ready in the saloon in ten minutes.

She then jumped out of bed, washed and put on her clothes and, because the sun was shining brightly through the porthole, she knew that it would be a very warm day.

She would not want the jacket she had left behind and the Macedonians, she thought, would find that a poor compensation for the large sum they had expected.

When she hurried up the companionway onto the deck, she found that the Marquis was waiting for her.

It was a very small Saloon built on the deck itself and there was, however, room for perhaps four people to eat at the table and, as there were only two of them, they sat opposite each other.

"You slept well, my darling?" the Marquis asked.

Because he was looking at her so lovingly, Lola felt her heart give a somersault.

"I dreamt of – you," she answered.

"That is what I hoped you would do."

He poured her out some coffee and she lifted the cover from her plate to find a delicious dish of eggs, bacon and tiny little sausages.

"Eat that all up," the Marquis urged her, "and then I will tell you what we are doing."

"I want to know first where we are and I suppose Signor Galvani owns this delightful little yacht."

"He had it specially made to carry him down the River Arno to Pisa, where we are now and, when you have finished your breakfast, we are going first to a very special appointment and then to my yacht, which is waiting for us in the Port."

"Your yacht!" Lola exclaimed.

"It was to be a surprise for you when we were ready to leave Italy," the Marquis said. "Having come here by train, I thought it would be amusing to go back by sea."

She was looking at him with excitement in her eyes and he added,

"I had expected sometime in the near future to be in Italy and I had already sent my yacht here to wait for me. So by good fortune everything has fitted in very neatly."

"You mean perfectly," Lola said. "Could anything you plan be less than perfection and that naturally includes – last night?"

She gave a little sigh.

"I could not imagine how you could possibly rescue me and then suddenly you appeared through the floor."

"Nothing could have been more fortunate than to have a Macedonian footman to tell me of its existence," the Marquis said. "His friends planned to use it as a way of escape if the police came to arrest them."

"I see and they must have been very astonished this morning when they found that I had used it to disappear."

"They may have thought you flew back to Heaven from where you had come," the Marquis smiled.

"You never said anything like that to me before," Lola whispered.

"It is the sort of thing I intend to say a great deal in the future. Hurry up and eat, we have to go ashore."

"I am ready," Lola replied, "except for my hat."

"Go and fetch it. You will need it."

Lola did as she was told and, when she joined the Marquis a few minutes later, he was standing on the deck looking a little impatient.

The yacht was made fast at a small quay and, when they stepped ashore, the Marquis led Lola to where there were a few houses.

Among them she saw the spire of a small Church.

She had expected to see a carriage and she thought that the Marquis was taking her to another part of the Port where his yacht would be waiting.

Then, as she neared the little Church, she remarked,

"It is rather like the Church where I was going to pray yesterday, but was kidnapped before I reached it."

"We shall reach *this* Church," the Marquis replied, "and it is, my darling, where we are going to be married."

Lola stopped still.

"Did you say," she asked in a small voice, "we are going to be – *married*?"

"I realised when I lost you," the Marquis said, "that I could not live without you and it is as simple as that."

He paused and then continued,

"We are very fortunate, my darling, in having here a man I was at Oxford with. He wrote a few months ago to tell me where he was after he had been ordained and I had intended, after my discussions with Galvani, to come and see him. Now Higgins has given him a letter saying that I want to be married, but it has to be kept a complete and absolute secret."

"I cannot – believe it," Lola said. "Are you quite, quite sure that you will not regret – marrying me?"

"I only have one thing I will regret," the Marquis replied, "and that is that I was stupid enough to upset you by offering you something else. It is not going to be easy, my precious, but if we are together and you love me as I love you, does anything else matter?"

Lola felt as if all the stars in the sky had fallen into her breast.

At the same time the sun was blinding her eyes.

The Marquis loved her, he really loved her.

In the same way her father had loved her mother and her mother had loved her father.

For a moment she could not speak, she only felt the wonder of love flowing over her.

She wanted to cry from sheer happiness.

The Marquis reached out and took her hand.

"What are we waiting for, my darling?" he asked. "I want you to be my wife."

He took her up the steps and through the door into the Church.

The candles on the altar were lit and a Priest in a white surplice was standing waiting for them.

The Marquis drew her forward and, as they reached him, the Priest started the Marriage Service.

He recited the beautiful words very sincerely.

Lola felt that her father and mother were there with them and they were happy because she had found the real love that had been theirs.

When she and the Marquis knelt for the Blessing, she was sure that the angels were singing in the Heavens and a burning light from God encircled them.

They signed the Marriage Register and the Priest, who was a good-looking young man, congratulated them both.

"I always hoped that Kelvin would find someone who would love him for himself," he said, "and was not blinded by his title or Queens Hoo."

"I promise I will look after him," Lola said.

"That is exactly what I wanted you to say," the Priest replied.

"We will come back and see you again before we return to England," the Marquis promised. "Now we are going on our honeymoon and it will take some time."

"Enjoy yourselves," the Priest smiled, "and thank you, Kelvin, for your generosity to my Church. A lot of deserving people in this Port will be thanking you tonight."

The Marquis nodded and they left the Church.

"We have only to walk a short distance to where my yacht is moored," he said.

"I think there are wings on my heels and I am now flying," Lola sighed.

The Marquis took her hand.

As he had said, it was only a little way to where his yacht, which seemed to Lola very impressive, was waiting for them.

They then went aboard and the Captain greeted the Marquis and Lola, addressing her as 'my Lady'.

When they went into the Saloon, there was a bottle of champagne ready for them.

"Higgins has told the Captain," the Marquis said, "that we were married very quietly before we left England because you were in mourning for your parents."

"So no one will ever know that we were married in that dear little Church – by that charming Priest who was at Oxford with you," Lola murmured.

"We can trust him to keep our secret and from now on, my precious one, there will be no more secrets and no more lies and we will face the world bravely."

Lola drew in her breath.

She was just about to tell him that he need not be so apprehensive about the future when the Marquis said,

"Drink a little more of your champagne and then I want to show you something below."

She wondered what it could be.

Putting out his hand, he drew her from the Saloon and down the companionway to a much broader passage than there had been in Signor Galvani's yacht.

They walked along it.

Lola knew that he must be taking her to the Master cabin and she was right.

He opened the door.

She saw that it was a very large and comfortable cabin with portholes on either side of it.

It was massed with flowers like those she had seen in Signor Galvani's beautiful garden and also in the garden at Queens Hoo.

"It is lovely, lovely," she said, "and I know that you love flowers as much as I do."

"They are like you," the Marquis said, "Only you are more beautiful, my darling, than the whitest lily and your lips are like rosebuds."

He pulled her into his arms as he spoke.

Now his kiss was not just possessive but passionate and demanding.

"I want you and I love you," he breathed. "Higgins will have told the Steward that we went to a very late party last night and we are therefore going to rest."

Lola looked at him and he added,

"It is not really a lie because what we had to do together last night was far more demanding than dancing a waltz!"

Lola laughed.

"You are twisting it round to suit yourself."

"What would suit me is to have you close in my arms and that means I don't want to wait any longer than I have waited already."

He moved towards the door and she knew that he was going to undress in another cabin.

Quickly she took off the gown she was wearing and then she saw, just as last night, Higgins had left one of her prettiest nightgowns on the bed.

'I am married, *I am married*,' Lola told herself.

As she moved her hands, she saw the wedding ring that the Marquis had given her flashing in the sunlight.

He had asked her to give back to him the simple gold ring he had lent her to wear when they left London for Italy.

And now she was certain that he had given her his mother's, which to him was sacred.

'Thank You God, thank You,' she murmured as she slipped between the sheets.

She felt once again that all the angels were singing overhead and her father and mother were smiling at her and blessing them both.

All her troubles were over.

She had found love, the real love, as they had done, and beside that nothing mattered in the whole wide world.

Then the Marquis came into the cabin.

He was wearing the same robe he had worn when he had come to her bedroom at Signor Galvani's and she had turned him away.

"I have just been thinking, my darling Kelvin," she said, "that I have a wedding present for you."

"I wish I could say the same," the Marquis replied. "But we are going to Greece and I am sure that I shall find something for you there which is worthy of the Goddess that you are."

"My present is rather different," Lola said, "but I think that it will make you happy."

"You do that already, but tell me what it is."

He sat down on the bed and he thought as he looked at his wife that no one could be so lovely.

No one could be more exquisite and ethereal.

"I love you," he said compulsively, "and I will fight with every nerve in my body to stop anyone from hurting or upsetting you."

He could not help thinking that it was not going to be very easy.

Yet because he loved her, he would, like a Knight in Shining Armour, protect her from any unpleasantness or difficulties that his family might create.

Lola held out her arms.

"My wedding present," she said, "is a very strange one. It is the name of my mother."

The Marquis looked at her in perplexity.

"The name of your mother?" he repeated. "That is something you have not yet told me."

"I know. You were curious, but I did not want you to find out because, if you had, you might have sent me away to live with my uncle whom I hate."

"You hate your uncle," the Marquis said, as if he was trying to work it out. "So that is the reason why you went to the Agency to find employment?"

"Yes, that is why," Lola agreed, "and Mrs. Hill sent me to you, which I am sure was by the guidance of Papa and Mama who just knew how unhappy I would have been with Uncle Arthur."

"Then who is he and exactly why should he make you unhappy?" the Marquis quizzed her.

There was a little pause and then Lola replied,

"He is the Earl of Kencombe and I thought perhaps that you might have met him."

The Marquis stared at her.

"I do know the Earl of Kencombe. Are you telling me that he is your uncle?"

"Mama was Lady Cecilia Combe and he was her elder brother. When she ran off to marry Papa, her father, who was then the Earl, disowned her and refused to have her name ever mentioned in his house."

The Marquis was looking at her with astonishment as she went on,

"Uncle Arthur was unkind too and only when Papa and Mama were killed in a train accident did he say that I would have to go and live with him and I just knew how unhappy it would make me."

"So you came to me," the Marquis murmured. "I can hardly believe it."

"But it is true," Lola said, "and because Mama gave up her family and everything as she loved Papa, who had been the Tutor to her younger brother, I wanted to be loved in the same way."

"That is how I love you, my darling. I have married you not knowing who you were and I would have married you if you had been the daughter of a crossing-sweeper!"

"I know it makes it easier for you and for me," Lola said, "that Mama was Lady Cecilia Combe."

"It makes it very much easier, because my great-grandfather married a Combe, so we are, my precious one, already related to each other!"

Lola laughed.

"It is all quite unbelievable. No one would believe that we have been through so much because you wanted an electric train."

"A Train to Love," the Marquis said, "which has brought you to me and I will never, my precious, beautiful, wonderful wife, lose you again. You are mine and I will kill anyone who attempts to take you from me."

"Do you think I could ever leave you?" Lola asked.

The Marquis put his arms round her and she moved closer to him.

"When you left me the other night," she whispered, "I wanted to tell you that I would do as you asked because I love you so much."

"You were right to refuse, Lola. It was very wrong of me to think for one moment that you were anything but good and pure."

His lips were against the softness of her skin as he added,

"That is what I always wanted from my wife and that is how we will bring up our children to be good and to want what is right and to find the same love that we have found."

Then he was kissing her again.

Kissing her so that Lola thought that they were both flying in the sky.

The Gates of Paradise were opening for them.

'I love you, I love you,' she wanted to say, but her heart was saying it for her.

She knew that the Marquis's heart was saying it as well.

This was love – real love – and it was theirs for Eternity and for ever.